Robert H. Derrah

Derrah's Official Street Railway Guide

for eastern Massachusetts and Rhode Island

Robert H. Derrah

Derrah's Official Street Railway Guide
for eastern Massachusetts and Rhode Island

ISBN/EAN: 9783337381288

Printed in Europe, USA, Canada, Australia, Japan

Cover: Foto ©Andreas Hilbeck / pixelio.de

More available books at **www.hansebooks.com**

DERRAH'S

Official
Street Railway Guide

For
Eastern Massachusetts and
Rhode Island

FOURTH EDITION

Boston:
The Lufkin Press, 145 High Street
1899

Introduction.

WITH thanks for the generous patronage of the past, the publisher of **Derrah's Street Railway Guide for Eastern Massachusetts** presents the fourth edition with a hope that it will meet with continued favor. The vast extent of the electric railway system of Eastern Massachusetts has rendered such a guide necessary to those who travel on the trolley cars for business or pleasure. Each year the Guide has grown, and in the present volume, in response to a general demand, new features have been embodied such as time-tables of the different suburban railways, etc. The descriptive matter, which was of especial interest to those planning trolley trips, showing what might be seen from the cars of the different lines, has been carefully revised, and much that is new has been incorporated. It is believed also that the new pictures and the enlarged map, which shows the existing and projected railways, will be appreciated, while all the old features, which have made the Guide popular in the past, have been retained. The Guide now tells how to reach every point on the electric lines radiating from the city of Boston, the distance, rates of fare, running time, time-tables, names of street railways, Boston night car service, where to take cars for different points from Boston, how to recover articles left in the cars, etc.

Not only on account of its completeness is this Guide believed to have a special value, but the publication may be regarded as official and authentic, the proofs having been corrected and revised by the officials of the various street railways described. The success of former editions is largely due to this fact, and the publisher wishes to thank all the street railway officials and others who have done so much to make this work popular among the patrons of the trolley.

In response to a general demand, the time-tables of the different suburban railway companies represented in this Guide are published this year for the first time. It would obviously be impossible to publish the running time of all cars on all the lines, even if it were desirable. The cars of the Boston Elevated Railway Company run so frequently on all lines that no attempt is made to give the schedules of that road, except for the night cars—a feature which has been found popular in past editions.

On the suburban roads the running time of the first car, together with the number of cars per hour, or the general running schedule, is given. This will enable any one to approximate the connections which may be made at any given point. While the time-tables have been revised by the officials of the different railway companies themselves, and are therefore the official time-tables, some mistakes may occur, owing to necessary changes, etc., but it is believed that they are substantially correct and may be relied upon, although the street railway companies or the author will not be held responsible for any changes, mistakes or delays that may occur.

Index to Contents.

Boylston Centre . . . . .
Bradley's Fertilizer from North Weymouth .
Braggville from South Framingham . .
Braintree . . . . . .
Braintree from Hingham . . . .
Bramanville from Worcester . . .
Bridgewater . . . . .
Brittania from Taunton . . . .
Brockton . . . . . .
Brockton from Mansfield . . .
Brockton Heights from Brockton . .
Brookfield from Worcester . . .
Brookville . . . . .
Campbello . . . . .
Caryville from So. Framingham . . .
Central from Forest Hills . . . .
Centredale from Providence . . .
Chartley . . . . . .
Chelmsford Centre from Lowell . . .
Chelsea . . . . . .
Chelsea from Boston . . . .
Chelsea from Everett . . . .
Chelsea from Malden . . . .
Chelsea from Melrose Highlands . . .
Cherry Valley from Worcester . . .
Clarendon Hills . . . . .
Clifton Heights . . . . .
Cliftondale from Lynn . . . .
Cliftondale from Malden . . . .
Clinton . . . . . .
Cochituate from Natick . . . .
Collinsville from Lowell . . . .
Conomo . . . . . .
Cranston from Providence . . . .
Danvers from Salem . . . .
Danvers Centre from Salem . . .
Danvers Centre from Beverly . . .
Danvers Square from Beverly . . .
Dedham . . . . . .
Dighton . . . . . .
Dodgeville . . . . . .
Dodgeville from Providence . . .
Dyerville from Providence . . . .
East Braintree from Braintree . . .
East Bridgewater . . . . .
East Bridgewater from Brockton . .
East Brookfield from Worcester . .
East Dedham . . . . .
East Dedham from Forest Hills . . .

Index to Descriptive Matter.

Index to Advertisers.

If a Parcel is Lost in the Cars of

THE	INQUIRY SHOULD BE MADE AT
Arlington & Winchester St. Ry.	Office, Wakefield, Mass.
Beverly & Danvers St. Ry.	Office, 333 Union St., Lynn.
Boston Elevated St. Ry.	Office, 101 Milk St., Boston.
Boston, Milton & Brockton St. Ry.	Office, Milton, Mass.
Braintree & Weymouth St. Ry.	Office, Weymouth Centre, Mass.
Bridgewater, Whitman & Rockl'd St. Ry.	Office, North Abington, Mass.
Brockton St. Ry.	Office, Main Street, Brockton.
Brockton, Bridgewater & Taunt'n St. Ry.	Office, Bridgewater, Mass.
Brockton & East Bridgewater St. Ry.	Office, Bridgewater, Mass.
Commonwealth Ave. St. Ry.	Office, Walnut St., Newtonville.
Dartmouth & Westport St. Ry.	Office, Purchase St., N. Bedford.
Dighton, Somerset & Swansea St. Ry.	Office, Taunton, Mass.
East Taunton St. Ry.	Office, 23 Sumer St., Taunton,
Exeter, Hampton & Amesbury St. Ry.	Office, Exeter, N. H.
Fitchburg & Leominster St. Ry.	Office, Fitchburg, Mass.
Fitchburg & Suburban St. Ry.	Office, Leominster, Mass.
Framingham Union St. Ry.	Office, So. Framingham, Mass.
Fram'ham, Southboro & Marlboro St. Ry.	Office, Northboro, Mass.
Globe St. Ry.	Office, Fall River, Mass.
Gloucester St. Ry.	Office, Gloucester, Mass.
Gloucester, Essex & Beverly St. Ry.	Office, Essex, Mass.
Gloucester & Rockport St. Ry.	Office, Gloucester, Mass.
Hanover St. Ry.	Office, Hingham, Mass.
Haverhill, Georgetown & Danvers St. Ry.	Office, Georgetown, Mass.
Haverhill & Amesbury St. Ry.	Office, Merrimac, Mass.
Hingham St. Ry.	Office, Hingham, Mass.
Interstate St. Ry.	Office, No. Attleboro, Mass.
Leominster & Clinton St. Ry.	Office, Leominster, Mass.
Lowell, Lawrence & Haverhill St. Ry.	Office, Lawrence, or Supt's Office, Haverhill.
Lowell & Suburban St. Ry.	Receiving Office, Merrimac Sq., Lowell, Mass.
Lynn & Boston Ry.	Supt's Office, 214 Broadway, Chelsea; cor. Salem and Ferry Sts., Malden; Central Sq., Lynn; or Supt's Office, cor. Essex and Washington Sts., Salem, Mass.
Mansfield & Easton St. Ry.	Office, Norton, Mass.
Mansfield & Norton St. Ry.	Office, Norton, Mass.
Marlboro St. Ry.	Office, Marlboro, Mass.
Milford, Holliston & Framingham St. Ry.	Office, Milford, Mass.
Mystic Valley St. Ry.	Office, Wakefield, Mass.

If a Parcel is Lost in the Cars of

THE	INQUIRY SHOULD BE MADE AT
Nashua St. Ry.	Receiver's Office, East Pearl St., Nashua, N. H.
Natick & Cochituate St. Ry.	Office, Natick, Mass.
Needham & Boston St. Ry.	Office, Car Station, Washington St., Roslindale, Mass.
New Bedford, Middleboro & Brockton St. Ry.	Office, Middleboro, Mass.
Newburyport & Amesbury St. Ry.	Office, Newburyport, Mass.
Newport & Fall River St. Ry.	Office, Portsmouth, R. I.
Newton St. Ry.	Office, Car Station, Washington St., W. Newton, Mass.
Newton & Boston St. Ry.	Office, Newtonville, Mass.
Newtonville & Watertown St. Ry.	Office, Newtonville, Mass.
Norfolk Central St. Ry.	Office, Car Station, Dedham.
Norfolk Southern St. Ry.	Office, Westwood, Mass.
Norfolk Suburban St. Ry.	Office, cor. River St. and Hyde Park Ave., Hyde Park.
Norfolk Western St. Ry.	Office, Westwood, Mass.
North Woburn St. Ry.	Office, No. Woburn, Mass.
Norton & Attleborough St. Ry.	Office, Norton, Mass.
Norton & Taunton St. Ry.	Office, Norton, Mass.
People's St. Ry.	Office, Lawrence, Mass.
Providence & Taunton St. Ry.	Office, Rehoboth, Mass.
Quincy & Boston St. Ry.	Office, City Sq., Quincy, Mass.
Randolph St. Ry.	Office, City Sq., Quincy, Mass.
Reading & Lowell St. Ry.	Office, Wakefield, Mass.
Rockland & Abington St. Ry.	Office, No. Abington, Mass.
South Middlesex St. Ry.	Office, So. Framingham, Mass.
Taunton St. Ry.	Office, Union Block, Taunton.
Union Ry. (Providence, R. I.)	Office, Providence, R. I.
Union St. Ry. (New Bedford.)	Office, New Bedford, Mass.
Wakefield & Stoneham St. Ry.	Office, Wakefield, Mass.
Warren, Brookfield & Spencer St. Ry.	Office, Brookfield, Mass.
Wellesley & Boston St. Ry.	Office, Newtonville, Mass.
West Roxbury & Roslindale St. Ry.	Office, Car Station, Washington St., Roslindale, Mass.
Woburn & Reading St. Ry.	Office, Wakefield, Mass.
Worcester Consolidated St. Ry.	Office, Worcester, Mass.
Worcester & Marlboro St. Ry.	Office, Northboro, Mass.
Worcester & Clinton St. Ry.	Office, Boylston Centre, Mass.
Worcester & Suburban St. Ry.	Office, 43 Park St., Worcester.

It is quite important in applying for lost parcels to give the date, time (as near as possible,) and the route of the car on which you supposed the parcel was lost, as well as a full and accurate description of the same.

Boston Elevated Railway Company.

A PERSON IN BOSTON CAN GET A CAR

FOR	AT
Albany Depot, . . .	Union Station, Haymarket Sq., Post Office Sq., Park Sq., Rowe's Wharf, East Boston Ferry, Chelsea Ferry, South Station and Washington St., north of Essex St.
Allston, ...	Take through subway car at Union Station (and change at Park St. Station, Subway for Allston car), Bowdoin Sq. and Copley Sq.
Arlington, . . . , .	Bowdoin Sq., Park St. and Boylston St. Stations, Subway, Copley Sq.
Arlington Heights, . .	Same as Arlington.
Arnold Arboretum, .	Take a Jamaica Plain or Forest Hills car.
Ashmont, ...	Same as Milton.
Back Bay Fens, . . .	Take a Brookline, Reservoir, Allston, Oak Sq., Newton or Longwood car at Park St. and Boylston St. Stations, Subway.
Baldwin Street, East Cambridge, . . .	Same as East Cambridge.
Beachmont (Lynn & Boston R. R.)	Scollay Sq., Adams Sq., and Haymarket Sq. Stations, Subway.
Brighton, via Cambridge, ...	Bowdoin Sq.
Brighton, via Coolidge's Corner, ...	Take through Subway car at Union Station (and change at Park St. Station, Subway, for Brighton car), Copley Sq.
Broadway, Cambridge,	Park St. and Boylston St. Stations, Subway, Bowdoin Sq., Copley Sq. or Park Sq. and by transfer at West Boston Bridge.

A PERSON IN BOSTON CAN GET A CAR

FOR	AT
Brookline, (Cypress St.)	Park St. and Boylston St. Stations, Subway, East Boston Ferry, Copley Sq. and Washington St., north of Boylston St.
Bunker Hill Monument, ...	Albany Depot, Subway Stations, Post Office Sq., Adams Sq., Haymarket Sq., Union Station or on Washington St., north of Essex St.
Central Square, Cambridge, ...	Park St. and Boylston St. Stations, Subway, Bowdoin, Scollay, Adams and Copley Sqrs.
Charlestown Neck, Charlestown,	Subway Stations, Post Office, Adams, and Haymarket Sqrs. and Washington St.
Chelsea Ferry, . . .	Park, Post Office, Adams Sqrs., and Washington St., north of Boylston St.
Chelsea Sq., Chelsea (Lynn & Bos'n R R)	Scollay, Adams and Haymarket Sq. Stations, Subway.
Chestnut Hill and Reservoir, ...	Take through Subway car at Union Station (and change at Park St. Station, Subway, for Reservoir car), and Copley Sq.
City Point, So. Boston.	Union Station, Subway Stations, Albany Depot, South Station, Washington St., Haymarket, Post Office and Park Sqrs.
City Sq , Charlestown,	Albany Depot, Haymarket Sq., Post Office Sq., Washington St. All Subway Stations.
Clarendon Hill, Somerville, ...	Columbus Av., Park, Scollay, Haymarket Sqrs., Subway Stations and Union Station.
Columbus Avenue, . .	Union Station, Subway Stations, Albany Depot, Chelsea Ferry, Post Office Sq., Washington St. north of Boylston St.
Coolidge's Corner,	Same as Allston.
Cottage Farm Station,	Take Newton car via Commonwealth Ave. at Park and Boylston St. Stations, Subway, Copley Sq.

A PERSON IN BOSTON CAN GET A CAR

FOR	AT
:rescent Beach (Lynn & Boston R. R.) . .	Scollay, Adams and Haymarket Sq. Stations, Subway.
)avis Sq., Somerville, .	Subway Stations, Park and Scollay Sqrs.
)udley St., Roxbury,	Union Station, South Station, Subway Stations, East Boston Ferry, Rowe's Wharf, Copley Sq., Franklin St. and Washington St.
:ast Boston Ferry, . .	Park, Post Office and Adams Sqrs., Albany Depot, South Station, Union Station, and Washington St.
:ast Cambridge, . . .	Post Office, Adams and Scollay Sqrs., South Station, Washington St. north of Summer St.
:verett Sq., Everett, .	Subway Stations, Washington St., north of Broadway Ext.
:ield's Corner, . . .	Same as Upham's Corner.
:ield's Corner, via Dorchester Ave., . . .	Union Station, Adams Sq., Post Office Sq., Franklin St., South Station.
:orest Hills, ...	Union Station, Subway Stations, Chelsea Ferry, Rowe's Wharf, East Boston Ferry, South Station, Albany Depot, Park, Copley Sqrs., and Washington St.
:orest Hills Cemetery,	Same as Forest Hills.
:ranklin Field, . . .	Union Station, Subway Stations, and Washington St.
:ranklin Park, . . .	Union Station, Subway Stations, Copley Sq., Washington St., and by transfer at Dudley St. and Grove Hall.

A PERSON IN BOSTON CAN GET A CAR

FOR	AT
Franklin St., Som'ville,	Subway Stations, Post Office, Adams and Haymarket Sqrs., and Washington St.
Grove Hall, ...	Union Station, Subway Stations, Park and Copley Sqrs., and Washington St.
Harvard College, . .	Same as Harvard Sq.
Harvard Sq., Camb'ge,	Bowdoin Sq., Park St. and Boylston St. Stations, Subway, Post Office, Park, Copley and Haymarket Sqrs. (Union Station by transfer at Craigie Bridge.)
Highland Ave., Somerville, ...	Same as Clarendon Hill.
Huntington Ave., Mechanics Building, . .	Take through Subway car at Union Station (and change at Park St. Station, Subway for Huntington Ave. car), Subway Stations, Park and Copley Sqrs.
Jamaica Plain, . . .	Union Station, Subway Stations, and Copley Sq.
Longwood Ave., . .	Same as Huntington Avenue.
Magoun Sq., Somerville	Subway Stations and Union Station.
Malden, ...	Subway Stations and Union Station.
Marine Park, So. Boston	Take South Boston or City Point car at Union Station, South Station, Subway Stations, Post Office Sq., Park Sq., and Washington St.
Marlborough St., . .	Copley Sq., Charles and Beacon Sts.
Medford, ...	Subway Stations and Union Station.

A PERSON IN BOSTON CAN GET A CAR

FOR	AT
Meeting House Hill, .	Union Station, Park St. and Boylston St. Stations, Subway, Copley Sq. and Washington St.
Middlesex Fells, Medford, ...	Take Medford or Malden car via West Everett at Subway Stations and Union Station.
Milton, ...	Union Station, Subway Stations, Haymarket Sq., Post Office Sq., or take Field's Corner or Neponset car and by transfer at Park St. (Dor.)
Mount Auburn, Cambridge, ...	Park St. and Boylston St. Stations, Subway, and Copley Sq., and by transfer at Harvard Sq.
Maplewood, ...	Scollay, Adams, and Haymarket Sq. Stations, Subway.
Mount Pleasant, . . .	Same as Upham's Corner.
Navy Yard, Charlestown, ...	Take any Bunker Hill or Chelsea car.
Neponset, ...	Union Station, all Subway Stations, Franklin St., or take Field's Corner or Milton car and by transfer at Park St. (Dor.)
Newton, ...	Take through Subway car at Union Station, (and change at Park St. Station, Subway, for Newton car), Subway Stations, Bowdoin, Scollay, Park or Copley Sqrs. and by transfer at Harvard Sq.
Newton Boulevard, .	Take through Subway car at Union Station (and change at Park St. Station, Subway, for Newton Boulevard car), Copley Sq.
Norfolk House, . . .	Union Station, Park St. and Boylston St. Stations, Subway, Haymarket, Adams and Copley Sqrs. and Washington St.

A PERSON IN BOSTON CAN GET A CAR

FOR | AT

Norfolk St., Dorchester, — Washington St. south of Franklin St. or by transfer at Dudley St. and Grove Hall.

North Cambridge, . . — Bowdoin Sq., Park St. and Boylston St. Stations, Subway, and Copley Sq.

Oak Square, ... — Same as Allston route, or take Newton car from Park St. and Boylston St. Stations, Subway, Bowdoin or Copley Sqrs.

Pearl St., Cambridgp't, — Park St. and Boylston St. Stations, Subway, Bowdoin, Park and Copley Sqrs.

Porter's Station, Cambridge, ... — Bowdoin Sq., Park St. and Boylston St. Stations, Subway, Copley Sq.

Post Office Square, . . — Union Station, South Station, Albany Depot, Columbus Av., Park Sq., or any place on Washington St.

Providence Depot, . . — All Steam Railroad Stations, Subway Stations, Bowdoin and Post Office Sqrs., Rowe's Wharf, East Boston Ferry, Chelsea Ferry, and Washington St., north of Eliot St.

Revere, ... — Scollay, Adams and Haymarket Sq. Stations, Subway.

Rowe's Wharf, . . . — Union Station, East Boston Ferry, Park Sq., Tremont St. south of Eliot, Washington St. south of Summer, and Albany Depot.

Roxbury Crossing, . . — Rowe's Wharf, Union Station, South Station, East Boston Ferry, Subway Stations, and Washington St.

Spring Hill, Somerville, — Park St. and Boylston St. Stations, Subway, Copley, Bowdoin, Adams and Haymarket Sqrs., and Washington St. north of Boylston St.

South Station, . . . — Union Station, Chelsea Ferry, East Boston Ferry, Rowe's Wharf, and Washington St.

A PERSON IN BOSTON CAN GET A CAR

FOR	AT
Union Sq., Somerville,	South Station, Union Station, Copley, Park, Haymarket and Bowdoin Sqrs., and Washington St. north of Summer St.
Union Station, . . .	Steam Railroad Station, Subway Stations, and on all the principal streets.
Upham's Corner, . .	Union Station, Subway Stations, Copley Sq., Franklin St., Washington St., and Huntington Ave., north of Massachusetts Ave.
West Everett, . . .	Subway Stations and Union Station.
Winter Hill, Somerville,	Subway Stations, Albany Depot, Washington St., north of Essex St., Post Office and Adams Sqrs., Union Station.
Woodlawn Cemetery, .	Scollay, Adams and Haymarket Sq. Stations, Subway.
Waverley, ...	Park St. and Boylston St. Stations, Subway, Copley Sq.

NORUMBEGA PARK, from Boston: Take a Newton Boulevard car at Park St. and Boylston St. Stations, Subway, and Copley Sq., and change at the Newton line to cars of the Commonwealth Ave. St. Ry. Co., which run direct to the Park. 11 1-2 miles; time, 1 hour: fare, 10 cents. This line connects with cars running to all parts of the Newtons; also to Echo Bridge, Highlandville, Needham, Natick and all lines south and west of Auburndale.

NIGHT CARS

BOSTON ELEVATED RAILWAY COMPANY.

Cars Leave	For	First Car.	Last Car	Leaves
Adams Sq.,	Allston....................	*12.15	5.15	30 min earlier
"	Arlington Heights,.........	*12.30	4.30	60 " "
"	Brookline Village,.........	†1.00	4.45	20 " "
"	City Point, So. Boston,....	*12.30	5.30	30 " "
"	Clarendon Hill,...........	†1.15	4.15	37 " "
"	Dorchester, via Grove Hall,	‡12.30	5.30	40 " "
"	Dorchester (Field's Corner)	*1.00	5.00	35 " "
"	East Boston Ferry,........	*1.40	4.40	
"	East Cam. (Prospect St.)..	*12.15	5.15	25 " "
"	Also by Clarendon Hill			
	Route..............	†1.15	4.15	
"	Everett, (East)	*12.30	4.30	35 " "
"	Forest Hills, ...	†12.37	5.37	37 " "
"	Grove Hall, Warren St....	*12.30	5.30	30 " "
"	Grove Hall, Blue Hill Ave..	*1.00	5.00	30 " "
"	Harvard Sq. (Cambridge)	*12.30	5.30	30 " "
"	Jamaica Plain, ··········	*12.35	5.00	35 " "
E. Boston Ferry,	Jamaica Plain, via Adams Sq.	*1.53	4.53	48 " "
Adams Sq.,	Malden, ...	*1.00	5.10	40 " "
"	Medford, via Winter Hill,.	*12.30	4.30	40 " "
"	Milton and Neponset......	*1.00	5.00	45 " "
"	Newton, via Allston,......	*12.15	5.15	45 " "
"	Newton, via Cambridge.....	*12.30	5.30	Same hour
"	Reservoir, via Brookline			35 min earlier
	village,............	†1.00	4.45	
"	Watertown, via Cambridge	*12.30	5.30	56 " "
"	West Everett,............	*1.00	5.10	30 " "
"	Winter Hill, (Somerville)..	*12.30	4.30	28 " "
North Ferry,	Winthrop Junction, ...	*12.55	4.50	37 " "

(*) Cars run every hour. (†) Cars run every hour and a quarter.
(‡) Cars run every 30 minutes.

BOSTON TO FITCHBURG

Via South Framingham and Worcester.

TRUNK-LINE AND BRANCHES.

From	To	Mileage		Rate of Fare		Run'g Time	
		Between Stations.	From Boston.	Between Stations.	From Boston.	Between Stations.	From Boston.
						Hr Min	Hr Min
Boston,	Watertown,		6½		5		48
Watertown,	Waltham,	3		5		20	
	Newton H'lds,	4		5		28	
	Newton Upper Falls,	5		5		37	
	Highlandville,	7		5		47	
	*Needham,	8		5		52	
	Prospect Hill,	3¾		5		30	
	Newton,	1	7½	5	5	05	53
Newton,	Newton Ctre.,	3½		5		30	
	Waltham,via W. Newton,	5		5		38	
	Waltham,via Bemis,	3¾		5		30	
	Bemis,	1¾		5		15	
	Prospect Hill,	5¼		5		38	
	Newton H'ld,	3½		5		22	
	Newton Upper Falls,	4½		5		31	
	Highlandville,	6½		5		41	
	*Needham,	7½		5		46	
Newtonville,	Newtonville,	1	8½	5	10	07	1 00
	Newton Ctre.,	2¼		5		20	
	Newton H'lds,	2½		5		15	
	Newton Upper Falls,	3½		5		30	
	Highlandville,	5½		5		42	
	*Needham,	6½		5		50	
	Waltham,	3		5		20	
West Newton,	West Newton,	1¼	10¾	5	10	17	1 15
Auburndale,	Auburndale,	1	11¾	5	10	04	1 19
Newton Lower Falls,	NewtonLower Falls,	1½	13¼	5	10	11	1 30
	Wellesley Hills,	1½	14¾	5	15	07	1 37

For Detail Time Table see pages 33, 34 and 35.

* Connects with cars for Wellesley, Natick, Spring Street, West Roxbury, Dedham, etc.

BOSTON TO FITCHBURG

Via South Framingham and Worcester—Continued.

TRUNK-LINE AND BRANCHES.

From	To	Mileage. Between Stations.	Mileage. From Boston.	Rate of Fare Between Stations.	Rate of Fare From Boston.	Run'g Time Between Stations. Hr Min	Run'g Time From Boston. Hr Min
Wellesley Hills,	**Wellesley,**	1½	16¼	5	15	08	1 45
Wellesley,	Needham,	3¼		5		15	
	Natick,	3	19¼	5	20	15	2 00
Natick,	South Natick,	2		5		15	
	Felchville,	1½		5		7	
	North Natick,	2		5		15	
	Cochituate,	3		5		20	
	Saxonville,	5		10		30	
	So.Framingham	4	23¼	5	25	30	2 30
So. Framingham	Mass. State Militia Grounds	1½		5		08	
	Saxonville,	4		5		30	
	Holliston,	5		5		25	
	Braggville,	9		10		45	
	Milford,	12		15		1 00	
	Hopedale,	14¼		15		1 16	
	*Caryville,	17		25		1 27	
	*West Medway	18		25		1 35	
	*Medway,	19½		25		1 45	
	Ashland,	3		5		21	
	Hopkinton,	7		10		39	
	Framingham,	2	25¾	5	30	15	2 45
Framingham,	**Fayville,**	2¾	28	5	35	20	3 05
Fayville,	**Southboro,**	3¼	31¼	5	40	20	3 25
Southboro,	**Marlboro,**	3½	34¾	5	45	18	3 43
Marlboro,	Hudson,	4		5		20	
	Northboro,	5½	40½	10	55	30	4 13
Northboro,	Westboro,	4⅕		5		30	
	Shrewsbury,	5	45¼	5	60	30	4 43
Shrewsbury,	**Lake Quinsigmond**	3	48½	5	60	15	4 58
Lake Quinsigmond	**Worcester,**	2½	51	5	65	30	5 28
Worcester,	Grafton, Millbury,	6½		10		40	

For Detail Time Tables see pages 33, 34 and 35.

*Change cars at Milford for these points.

BOSTON TO FITCHBURG

Via South Framingham and Worcester — Continued.

TRUNK-LINE AND BRANCHES.

From	To	Mileage. Between Stations.	From Boston.	Rate of Fare Between Stations.	From Boston.	Run'g Time Between Stations.	From Boston.	
						Hr Min	Hr Min	
Worcester,	Bramanville,	8		10		50		
	Wilkinsonville,	8¾		15		52		
	Saundersville,	9¾		15		1 00		
	Farnumsville,	11⅓		20		1 10		
	Rockdale,	13		25		1 20		
	Valley Falls,	4		5		32		
	Cherry Valley,	4½		10		38		
	Leicester,	7		10		49		
	Spencer,	12		20		1 18		
	†E. Brookfield,	15¼		25		1 30		
	No. Brookfield,	19½		30		2 00		
	Brookfield,	18¾		30		1 55		
	W. Brookfield,	21¾		35		2 11		
	Warren,	25¼		45		2 27		
	W. Warren,	27½		40		2 39		
	Boylston Centre,	7	58	10	75	30	5 58	
Boylston Centre,	Clinton,	5	63	10	85	30	6 28	
Clinton,	So. Lancaster,	3	69	5	90	15	6 43	
So. Lancaster,	Lancaster,	1½	70½	5	90	10	6 53	
Lancaster,	No. Village,	1½	72	5	90	05	6 58	
No. Village,	Leominster Park,	3	75	5	95	15	7 13	
Leominster Park,	Leominster,	3	78	5	1 00	15	7 28	
Leominster,	So. Fitchburg,	2¾	80¾	5	1 05	15	7 43	
	No. Leominster,	1⅛		5		15		
	Fitchburg via No. Leominster Whalom Park }	6¾		5		45		
		4		5		20		
‡Fitchburg,	Fitchburg,	2	82¾	5	1 05	15	7 58	
	W. Fitchburg,	2½		5		23		
	Whalom Park,	3¼		5		23		

(side note: For Detail Time Tables see pages 33, 34 and 35.)

A line also runs from Worcester to No. Grafton and Grafton. Fare to No. Grafton, 10 cents; to Grafton, 15 cents. The distance to Grafton is 9 miles.

A line will soon be in operation from Worcester to Webster, via Auburn, Learnedville, No. Oxford, Oxford, and East Village. See Map.

†Change cars for North Brookfield.

‡Round trip tickets over 25 mile ride at reduced prices.

TIME-TABLE.

Boston to Fitchburg.

CARS LEAVE	FOR	AT
Boston.............	Watertown about every 5 minutes.	
Watertown	Waltham and Auburndale, 6.30, *8.30, then every 30 minutes until 11.30. Return Auburndale, 6.15, 6.45, *8.15, then every 30 minutes until 10.45.	
	Needham, via Newtonville, Newton Highlands, Newton Upper Falls and Highlandville, 6.17, then every 20 minutes until 11.57. Return leave Needham, 6.00 then every 20 minutes until 11.50 p. m.	
Newton	Newtonville, Newton Highlands, Upper Falls and Needham, 7 minutes later than Watertown. Return leave Needham at 6.00, then every 20 minutes until 11.50 p. m.	
	Newton Centre, 6.35, then every 30 minutes until 11.35 p. m. Return 6.35, then every 30 minutes until 11.35 p. m.	
	Waltham via West Newton, 6.30, 7.00, 7.30, *8.45, then every 15 minutes until 11.30 p. m. Return 6.22, 6.42, 7.08, 7.38, *8.08, then every 15 minutes until 11.23.	
	West Newton, and Newton Lower Falls, 6.22 due, then every 15 minutes until 9.52 p. m., then 10.22, 10.52 and 11.22. Return, leave Newton Lower Falls same time.	
	Waltham via Bemis, 6.45, then hourly until 1.45, *8.45, then every 30 minutes until 11.15 p. m. Return 6.10, 7.15, then hourly until 2.15, then every 30 minutes until 11.15, *8.15.	
Newtonville	Newton Centre, 7 minutes later then Newton. Return same time as for Newton.	
	Newton Highlands, Upper Falls, Highlandville and Needham. 6.10 a. m. then every 20 minutes until 11.30 p. m., then 12.10.	
Newton Lower Falls	Natick, 7.07. *8.08 a.m., then every 30 minutes until 10.07 p. m., then 10.47. Return, 7.35. 8.06, *8.36, then every 30 minutes until 10.36 p. m., then 11.16.	
Natick	South Natick, 6.20, 8.25, then hourly until 1.05, 1.50, then every 30 minutes until 10.10 p. m., then 11.10. Return 6.35, 8.40, then hourly until 1.20, then every 30 minutes until 9.56, 10.25.	
	Cochituate, 6.35, *9.00 a. m., then every 30 minutes until 10.37 p. m. Return 6.05, *8.35 a. m., then about every 30 minutes until 10.19 p. m.	
	Saxonville, 7.00, 9.00 a. m., then hourly until 1.37 p. m., then hourly until 9.37, 10.05 p. m. Return 6.55, 8.23 a. m., then hourly until 1.07, then hourly until 10.07.	
	South Framingham, 6.24, 8.13 a. m., then hourly until 7.13, then every 30 minutes until 7.13 p. m., then hourly until 10.13. Return 6.25, 8.43 a. m., then hourly until 1.13 p. m., then every 30 minutes, 8.13, 9.13, 6.43, 10.43.	

*First car Sunday.

TIME-TABLE.

Boston to Fitchburg — Continued.

CARS LEAVE	FOR AT
So. Framingham ...	Ashland and Hopkinton, 6.44, *8.37, then hourly until 3.07, then every 30 minutes until 8.07, then 9.07, 9.37, 10.38. Return 5.48, 8.03, then hourly until 2.32, then every 36 minutes until 9.02, 10.02.
	Holliston, Milford and Hopedale, 6.35, 8.35 a. m. and every 30 minutes until 9.35 p. m., then 10.08, 10.35, 11.05. Return, leave Hopedale, 6.20, *7.20, and every 30 minutes until 9.20 p. m., 10.20. Cars run more frequently and later Saturday and Sunday evenings.
Milford	Caryville, West Medway and Medway, 6.05, *7.35 a. m., then every 45 minutes until 6.50 due, then 8.20, 9.50. Return 6.05, *8.20 a. m., then every 45 minutes until 7.35 p. m., 9.05, 10.35. Cars run more frequently and later Saturday and Sunday Evenings.
So. Framingham ...	Marlboro via Framingham Centre, Fayville, Southboro, 6.42, 7.07, 7.45, 8.00, then every 30 minutes until 9.30 p. m., then 10.10, 10.35. Return, leave Marlboro, 6.00, *7.00 a. m., then every 30 minutes until 10.00 p. m.
Marlboro	Hudson, 5.50, 7.30 a. m., then every 30 minutes until 10.00 p. m. Return 6.00, 6.30, 7.05, 8.05 a. m., then every 30 minutes until 10.05 p. m.
	Worcester via Northboro and Shrewsbury, 6.30, *7.30 a.m., then every hour until 9.30, then every 30 minutes until 9.30 p. m. (10.00, 10.30, 11.00, 11.30, runs to Northboro). Return, leaves Worcester, 7.00, *8.00 a. m., then hourly until 10.00, then every 30 minutes until 10.00 p. m. (10.30, 11.00, runs to Northboro only.)
Northboro	Westboro, 6.00, 7.00 a. m., then hourly untill 10.00 p. m. Return 30 minutes later.
Worcester	Spencer every 40 minutes.
Spencer	West Warren via Brookfield and Warren, 6.00, *7.00, then every 40 minutes until 10.20 p. m. Return, West Warren, 6.20, *7.00 a. m., then every 40 minutes until 9.40 p. m.
East Brookfield	North Brookfield, *6.40, 7.20, 8.00, then every 40 minutes until 10.40 p. m. Return *7.00 a. m., then every 40 minutes until 11. p. m.
Worcester	Leicester every 20 minutes.
	Rockdale via Bramanville, Wilkinsonville, Saundersville and Farnumsville, every 30 minutes.
	Grafton, via North Grafton, 1.15, 6.00, 7.00, then every 45 minutes until 10.00, then 11.00 p. m. Return same time.
	Clinton via Boylston Centre, 6.55, *8.25 a. m., then every 30 minutes until 9.55 p. m., then (10.25, 11.55 to Boylston Centre only.) Return leave Clinton *8.10, then 15 minutes later.
Clinton.	Leominster via Lancaster, 5.55, 7.00, *8.00 a. m., then hourly until 11.00, and then every 30 minutes until 10.30 p. m. Return leave Leominster same time until 10.00 p. m.
Leominster.	Fitchburg via S. Fitchburg, 6.30 a. m., then every 30 minutes until 12.30 p. m., then every 15 minutes until 9.45, then every 30 minutes until 11.30. Return leave Fitchburg 30 minutes earlier.

*First car Sunday.

TIME-TABLE.

Boston to Fitchburg—Continued.

CARS LEAVE	FOR	AT
Leominster	Fitchburg via No. Leominster and Whalom Park. 6.45 a. m., then every 30 minutes until 1.00 p. m., then every 15 minutes until 10.15. p. m. Return leave Fitchburg 6.15 a.m., then every 30 minutes until 1.00, then every 15 minutes until 10.15 p. m.	
Fitchburg...........	West Fitchburg, 6.00 a. m., then every 15 minutes until 11.00 p. m. Return same time.	
	Whalom, 6.45 a. m., then every 30 minutes until 1.00 p. m., then every 15 minutes until 10.53 p. m.	

BOSTON TO GLOUCESTER AND ROCKPORT

Via Lynn, Salem and Beverly.

TRUNK-LINE AND BRANCHES.

From	To	Mileage Between Stations	Mileage From Boston	Rate of Fare Between Stations	Rate of Fare From Boston	Run'g Time Between Stations	Run'g Time From Boston
						Hr Min	Hr Min
Boston,	Chelsea,			2½	5		16
Chelsea,	Woodlawn Cem	2½		5			14
	Beachmont,	3½		5			26
	Everett,	1²⁄₃		5			12
	Malden,	3⅓		5			22
	Melrose High's	6⅔		10			42
	Stoneham,	8²⁄₃		10		1 00	
	Woburn,	13¼		15		1 27	
	Melrose,	4		10			38
	Revere,	4	6½	5	5	19	35
Revere,	Lynn,	3½	10	5	10	25	1 00
Lynn,	Cliftondale,	4		5			32
	Beach Bluff,	4		5			22
	East Saugus,	2½		5			22
	Swampscott,	1½		5			15
	Marblehead,	6		10			45
	South Peabody	4		10			30
	Peabody,	6		10			40
	Wyoma Lake or Wyoma Village	2½		5			17
	North Saugus,	5½		10			35
	Saugus Centre,	3½		5			32
	Oaklandale,	4½		5			37
	Franklin Park,	4		5			35
	Malden,	9		10			52
	Melrose High's	11		15		1 00	
	Stoneham,	12		15		1 09	
	Woburn,	16		20		1 30	
	Lynnhurst,	3½		15			22
	Wakefield,	9		15			52
	Nahant Beach,	½		5			7
	Salem,	6	16	5	15	52	1 52
Salem,	Marblehead,	4½		5			34
	South Peabody,	4½		5			25

For detail Time Tables see pages 38, 39 and 40.

BOSTON TO GLOUCESTER AND ROCKPORT

Via Lynn, Salem and Beverly—Continued.

TRUNK-LINE AND BRANCHES.

From	To	Mileage. Between Stations.	From Boston.	Rate of Fare Between Stations.	From Boston.	Run'g Time Between Stations.	From Boston.
						Hr Min	Hr Min
Salem,	Peabody,	2½		5		20	
	Danvers,	4		5		26	
	Asylum Station	6		8		41	
	Putnamville,	7		8		45	
	Danvers Centre	6		8		41	
	Salem Willows	2		5		15	2 07
	Beverly,	2	18	5	20	15	
Beverly,	Putnamville,	9		10		1 15	
	Wenham,	6		5		31	
	Wenham Lake	3½		5		20	
	Peabody,	4		5		45	
	Beverly Cove,	2¼		5		11	
	Danvers Sq.	6		10		30	
	Danvers Centre	8		12		45	
	Asylum Station	8½		12		1 00	
	†Asbury Grove,	6½		10		38	
Longham,	**Longham,**	2	20	5	25	10	2 17
*Essex Falls,	**Essex Falls,**	6	26	5	30	30	2 47
Essex,	**Essex,**	1	27	5	30	05	2 52
Conomo,	**Conomo,**	1	28	5	35	05	2 57
West Gloucester,	**West Gloucester,**	2	30	5	35	10	3 07
Fernwood Lake,	**Fernwood Lake,**	3	33	5	40	15	3 22
Gloucester,	**Gloucester,**	2	35	5	40	10	3 32
	Riverdale,	1½		5		12	
	Bay View,	5		10		37	
	Annisquam,	3		5		25	
	Lanesville,	6½		10		45	
	Long Beach,	2½		5		12	
	East Gloucester or Rocky Neck	3		5		30	
	Rockport,	4	39	5	45	28	4 00
Rockport,	**Pigeon Cove,**	2½	41½	5	50	20	4 20

For detail Time Tables see pages 38, 39 and 40.

*A line of cars is run to Ipswich from Essex Falls; distance, 5 1-2 miles; running time 25 minutes; fare, 5 cents. †This line runs only as far as Wenham during winter.
About August 1st a line will probably be in operation from Ipswich to Georgetown and Newburyport via Rowley.

TIME - TABLE.

Boston to Gloucester and Rockport via Lynn and Salem.

CARS LEAVE	FOR		AT
Boston	Chelsea, Revere and Lynn, 6.00, 7.00, *7.37, 7.30, 8.00, then every 15 minutes until 8.15 p. m, then every 30 minutes until 11.15. Return, 6.30, *6.37, 7.00, then every 15 minutes until 7.15 p. m., then every 30 minutes until 10.15.		
Chelsea	Woodlawn Cemetery, 6.30, 7.05, then every 30 minutes until 11.35, then every 15 minutes until 6.35, then every 30 minutes until 11.35.		
	Beachmont, 6.15, 6.57, 7.07, 7.22, 7.37, then every 30 minutes until 2.37, then every 15 minutes until 7.07, then every 30 minutes 12.07 then 1.30 a. m.		
	Everett, 6.00, then every 30 minutes until 11.30 p. m.		
	Malden, 6.00, then every 15 minutes until 12.00 noon, 12.30, 1.00, then every 15 minutes until 9.30, then every 30 minutes until 12.00 midnight. Return, 5.35, then every 15 minutes until 11.35, 12.05, 12.35, then every 15 minutes until 9.05, then every 30 minutes until 11.35 p. m.		
	Melrose and Melrose Highlands, 6.00, then every 15 minutes until 9.30, then every 30 minutes until 12.00.		
	Stoneham, 6.00, 6.30, 7.00, then hourly until 12.00, then every 30 minutes until 10.00.		
	Woburn, same as Stoneham.		
	Revere, 6.00, 6.15, then about every 10 minutes until 7.11, then every 6 minutes until 11.07, then about every 10 minutes until 1.30 a. m. Return 5.15, 5.32, 5.43. Last car 11.35 p. m.		
Revere.	Lynn, 6.57, 7.27, 7.57, 8.27, then every 15 minutes until 8.12, then every 30 minutes until 11.42, 6.30, 7.00, 7.15, then every 15 minutes until 6.55, then every 30 minutes until 10.15 p. m.		
Lynn	Cliftondale, 6.43, 7.13, *8.43, then every 30 minutes until 10.43. Return 6.15, *8.15, then every 30 minutes until 10.15 p. m.		
	Beach Bluff, 7.30, 8.30, 9.30, then every 30 minutes until 12.00 m., then every 15 minutes until 7.30, then 8.00, 8.30, 9.30. Return 7.22, 8.07, 8.37, then 7 minutes later than from Lynn, (10.37, 11.37 p. m. Saturdays and Sundays only.)		
	East Saugus, 6.28, 6.43, then every 15 minutes until 10.58 p. m. Return 6.25 then every 15 minutes until 10.40 p. m.		
.	Swampscott, 6.30, *7.30, then every 15 minutes until 11.15, then 11.45, 12.15. Return 6.30 then every 15 minutes until 11.00, 11.30, 12.00 p. m.		
	Marblehead, 7.30, *8.30, 9.30, then every 30 minutes a. m., 15 minutes, p. m. until 7.30, then 8.00, 8.30, 9.30. Return 45 minutes later.		
	South Peabody. Same as Peabody.		
	Wyoma Lake, Wyoma Village, 6.05 and then at least every 15 minutes until 11.00 p. m., then 12.00, Return 5.40, 6.10, then every 15 minutes until 10.25 p. m. then 11.25.		

*First car Sunday.

TIME - TABLE.

Boston to Gloucester and Rockport via Lynn and Salem. — Continued.

CARS LEAVE	FOR	AT

Lynn . . . . North Saugus, same as Lynnhurst.

Saugus Centre, 6.28, *8.28, then every 30 minutes until 10.58 p. m. Return 6.15, 6.30, *8.00, then every 30 minutes until 10.30.

Peabody, about every 30 minutes.

Franklin Park, same as Malden.

Malden, same as Cliftondale. Return 6.15, *8.45, then every 30 minutes until 9.45 p. m.

Melrose Highlands, 6.28, *8.28, then every 30 minutes until 9.28. Return, 6.45, *8.45, then every 30 minutes until 9.45.

Stoneham, 6.28, *8.28, then every 30 minutes until 9.28.

Lynnhurst, 7.07, 7.37, 8.07, 9.07, *8.00, then every 30 minutes until 10.07 p.m. Return 6.30, 7.00, 7.30, 8.30, then every 30 minutes until 10.00 p. m.

Woburn, 6.28, *8.28, then every 30 minutes until 9.28.

Salem, 6.25, 7.02, then every 30 minutes until 1.02, then every 15 minutes until 6.32, then every 30 minutes until 9.32 p. m. Return 6.25, 7.00, 7.45, then every 30 minutes until 1.45, then every 15 minutes until 6.55, then every 30 minutes until 10.15 p. m. (10.45 Saturday and Sunday only.)

Salem . . . . Marblehead, 6.26, 6.56, a.m., *7.56, then every 30 minutes until 10.56. Return, 6.30 a. m., *8.00, then every 30 minutes until 10.30 p. m.

South Peabody, via No. Salem, 6.00, 6.30, 7.00, 7.30, 8.20, *8.50 a. m., then every 30 minutes until 10.20, (10.40 Sundays only), and 11.00 p. m. Return 6.30, 7.15, *9.15, then every 30 minutes until 9.45, 10.15, (10.40, not run Sunday), 10.45 and 11.15.

Peabody, 5.30, 6.15, *7.30, 7.05 and 8.15 a. m., (not run Sunday,) then every 15 minutes until 11.00 p. m. Return, 6.35, *7.50, then every 15 minutes until 11.20 p. m.

Danvers, 6.34, 7.04, 7.34, *8.04, then every 30 minutes until 10.34, 11.00. Return, 6.30, then every 30 minutes until 10.30 p. m.

Asylum Station, 6.34, 7.34, *8.34, then hourly until 10.34 p. m. Return 6.45, 7.15, *8.15, then hourly until 10.15 p. m.

Putnamville, 6.30, *7.30 a. m., then hourly until 10.30 p. m.

Salem Willows, 6.00, 6.25, 7.00, 7.40, 8.10, 8.40, *9.10 a. m., then every half hour until 10.10, then 11.00 p. m. Return 6.15, 6.42, 7.15, 8.05, 8.35, *9.05 a. m., then every hour until 10.35, then 11.15 p. m.

Danvers Centre, 7.04, *8.04, then hourly until 11.00 p. m. Return 6.14, 6.45, *7.45, then hourly until 9.45.

*First car Sunday.

TIME-TABLE.

Boston to Gloucester and Rookport via Lynn and Salem.—Continued.

Cars Leave	For	At

Salem ....

Wenham, 6.25, 6.55, 8.00, 9.00, 10.15, then hourly until 2.15, then every 30 minutes until 8.15, then hourly until 10.15, then 11.00 p. m. Return, 6.05, 6.35, 7.07, *8.07, 9.22 a. m., then hourly until 1.22, then 1.52, and every 30 minutes until 7.22, then 8.22, 9.22 and 10.07 p. m.

Beverly, 6.10, 6.25, 6.40, 9.55, 7.10, 7.25, 7.40, 7.55 *8.10 a. m., then every 15 minutes until 11.00 p. m. Return, via Cabot Street 6.10, 6.33, 6.47, 7.17, 7.47, 8.17, *8.47 a. m., then every 30 minutes until 10.17, then 10.47, to stable only. Via Rantoul Street, 7.37, 8.07, *8.37 a. m., then every 30 minutes until 10.37, then 11.27 p. m., to stable only.

Beverly ....

Putnamville, 7.05, 8.05, *9.05, then hourly until 10.05.

Peabody, via Rantoul Street, 7.37, *8.07, then every 30 minutes until 10.37. Via Cabot Street 6.10, 6.33, 6.47, 7.17, then every 30 minutes until 9.47, then 10.17, 10.47, *8.47.

Danvers, 7.00, *9.00 a. m., then hourly until 10.00 p. m. Return 6.30, *8.30 then hourly until 9.30.

Beverly Cove, 6.15, 6.50, *7.20, 8.00, 9.11, 10.11, then hourly until 11.11 p. m. Return, 6.30, 7.00, *7.30, 8.30, then hourly until 11.30.

Essex, Ipswich, and Gloucester, 7.00, *8.00, then every 30 minutes until 9.30 p. m., (10.00 p. m. to Essex and Ipswich), (11.00 to Essex). Return, leave Gloucester same time.

Essex Falls ....

§Ipswich, (Burnham's Corner) 6.10 a. m., *7.10, then every 30 minutes until 10.10 p. m. Return, leave Ipswich for Gloncester and Beverly, 7.00, *8.00 then every 30 minutes until 9.30 (10.00 to Beverly), (10.30, 11.00 to Essex Falls.)

‡Gloucester ....

Rockport and Pigeon Cove, 6.07 a. m., them every 30 minutes until 10.37, *8.07. Return, leave Pigeon Cove 6.22, then every 30 minutes until 11.22, *8.52.

East Gloucester or Rocky Neck, 6.37 a. m., then every 30 minutes until 12.15, then every 15 minutes until 8.15 p. m., *8.07. Return, 5.45, 6.30, then every 30 minutes until 10.10, *7.28, *8.00.

†Riverdale, Annisquam, Bay View and Lanesville, 5.30, 6.15, 7.00, 7.45, 8.30, then every 45 minutes until 10.45; Sundays, 7.15, 8.00, then every 45 minutes until 10.15. Leave Riverdale 16 minutes later. Return, leave Lanesville 6.15, 6.50, 7.45, then every 45 minutes until 11.00. Sundays, 8.00, then every 45 minutes until 11.30.

Long Beach, 7.00 a. m., then every 45 minutes until 8.07. Cars run every 15 minutes between these points on pleasant days.

*First car Sunday.   †Extra cars are run on pleasant days making a car every 22½ minutes.   ‡Centre Street.   §A line will probably be in operation about August 1st, from Ipswich to Georgetown and Newburyport via Rowley.

BOSTON TO NASHUA, N. H.,

Via Wakefield, Reading and Lowell.

TRUNK-LINE AND BRANCHES.

From	To	Mileage.		Rate of Fare		Run'g Time	
		Between Stations.	From Boston.	Between Stations.	From Boston.	Between Stations.	From Boston.
						Hr Min	Hr Min
Boston,	Everett,		5½		5		39
Everett,	Chelsea,						
	Revere,					10	
	Malden,	1	6½	5	5	22	59
Malden,	Chelsea,	3½		5		15	
	Medford,	2¼		5		30	
	Winchester,	5½		15			
	No. Woburn, } via Medford }	10½		10		1 00	
	Saugus Centre,	6		10		38	
	Franklin Park,	3		5		20	
	Cliftondale,	4		5		30	
	East Saugus,	5½		10		37	
	Lynn,	9		10		53	
	Revere,	5½		10		40	
	Beachmont,	7		10		47	
	Arlington via } Winchester }	8¾		20		57	
	Woburn, via } Medford, }	8		10		45	
Melrose Highlands,	Melrose Highlands, }	3	9½	5	10	12	1 11
	Chelsea,						
	Stoneham,	2½		5		22	
	Woburn,	6		10		45	
	Saugus Centre,	3		5		15	
	East Saugus,	4½		10		22	
	Lynn,	7		10		45	
Wakefield,	Wakefield,	3	12½	5	15	15	1 26
	Arlington via } Winchester }	8¾		10		55	
	Stoneham,	2½		5		15	
	Winchester,	5½		10		35	
	North Saugus,	2½		5		15	

For detail Time Tables see pages 43 and 44.

BOSTON TO NASHUA, N. H.,
Via Wakefield, Reading and Lowell.
Continued.

TRUNK-LINE AND BRANCHES.

From	To	Mileage.		Rate of Fare		Run'g Time	
		Between Stations.	From Boston.	Between Stations.	From Boston.	Between Stations. (Hr Min)	From Boston. (Hr Min)
Wakefield,	Lynnfield,	5½		10		30	
	Lynn,	9		5		54	
	So. Peabody,	8½		15		45	
	Salem,	13		20		1 15	
	Reading,	3	15½	5	15	15	1 41
Reading,	Arlington via Stoneham,	9¼		10		1 00	
	Stoneham,	3		5		20	
	Woburn,	5		5		30	
	Winchester, via Stoneham	6		10		40	
	Medford, via Woburn,	13		15		1 00	
	Medford, via Stoneham, Winchester.	10		15		55	
	Wilmington,	5½	21	5	20	29	2 10
Wilmington, Billerica Centre, No. Billerica, Nowell,	Billerica Centre,	7½	28½	10	30	38	2 48
	No. Billerica,	2	30½	5	35	15	3 01
	Lowell,	4	34½	5	40	16	3 22
	Tyngsborough,	7		10		45	
	Chelmsford Centre,	5		5		30	
	Wigginsville,	2		5		15	
	Tewksbury,	3½		5		30	
	Collinsville,	3¾		5		22	
	No. Chelmsford,	4¼		5		30	
	Pawtucketville,	2		5		20	
Dracut or Lakeview Park,	Dracut or Lakeview Park.	5	39½	5	45	25	3 47
	Nashua, N. H.	9	48½	15	60	47	4 34

For detail Time Tables see pages 43 and 44.

TIME-TABLE.

Boston to Nashua, N. H.

CARS LEAVE	FOR	AT
oston.............	Everett and Malden, about every 5 minutes.	
lalden.............	Melrose and Melrose Highlands, 5 minutes of and 25 past hour. Return, 15 minutes of and 15 minutes past the hour.	
elrose Highlands..	Wakefield, 6.45 a. m., then every 30 minutes until 11.15 p. m. Return 6.00 a. m., then every 30 minutes until 11.00 p. m.	
/akefield..........	Reading, 6.00 a. m., then every 30 minutes until 11.00 p. m. Return, 6.15 a. m., then every 30 minutes until 11.15 p. m.	
eading............	Billerica Centre, 7.15 a. m., then every 30 minutes until 7.15 p. m., then 8.15 and 9.15. Return 8.15, a. m., then every 30 minutes until 8.15 p. m., then 9.15 and 10.15.	
illerica Centre....	Lowell, 5.40, 7.15, 7.45, *8.15 a. m., then every 30 minutes until 10.15 p. m. Return 4.55, 6.30, 7.00, *7.30, then every 30 minutes until 10.15 p. m.	
/akefield..........	Stoneham, 5.30 a. m., then every 30 minutes until 11.00 p. m. Return 5.45 a. m., then every 30 minutes until 11.15 p. m.	
	North Saugus 6.00 a. m., then every 30 minutes until 10.00 p. m. Return 6.45, 7.15 a. m., then every 30 minutes until 10.45 p. m.	
	Lynnfield, 6.30, 7.30, 8.30, then every 30 minutes until 9.30 p. m. Return 6.30, 7.30, 8.30, 9.30, then every 30 minutes until 10.30 p. m.	
	So. Peabody, 6.30, 7.30, 8.30, 9.30, then every 30 minutes until 10.00 p. m. Return 6.15, 7.15, 8.15, 9.15, then every 30 minutes until 10.15 p. m.	
toneham..........	Winchester, 5.20, 5.50, 6.20, 7.35 a. m., then every 30 minutes until 10.35 p. m. Return one hour later.	
/inchester	Arlington, 5.40, 6.10, 6.40, 7.10, 7.55, then every 30 minutes until 10.55 p. m. Return 20 minutes later.	
eading............	Woburn, 6.15 a. m., then hourly until 1.15 p. m., then every 30 minutes until 9.15, 10.15 p. m. Return 6.45 a. m., then hourly until 1.45 p. m., then every 30 minutes until 9.45, then 10.45 p. m.	
	Stoneham, 5.00, 5.30, 6.00, 6.30, 7.15, then every 30 minutes until 10.15. Return 6.40, 7.10, 7.40, 8.10, 8.55, 9.25, then every 30 minutes until 11.55.	
owell	Chelmsford Centre, 5.15, 5.35, 6.15, 6.35, *8.05, then every 30 minutes until 10.35 p. m. Return 30 minutes later, *8.35.	
	Wigginsville, 5.26, 6.04, 6.24, 6.36, then 6.21, 36 and 51 minutes past hour until 10.51 p. m., then 11.10. *8.06. Return 5.45, 6.04, 6.24, 6.52, then 7.22, 37 and 52 minutes past hour until 10.52, *8.22.	
	Tewksbury, 5.20, 6.24, 7.06, then every 30 minutes until 10.36, *8.06. Return 5.50, 7.07, then every 30 minutes until 10.36 p. m., *8.36.	
	Nashua, N. H., 6.20, *7.35, then every 30 minutes until 10.20 p. m. Return 6.35, *8.05, then every 30 minutes until 10.35 p. m.	

*First car Sunday.

TIME TABLE.

Boston to Nashua, N. H.—Continued.

CARS LEAVE	FOR	AT
Lowell	Collinsville, 6.00, 6.20, 6.35, 6.50, *7.50, then every 30 minutes until 10.50 p. m., †10.50, ‡11.10. Return 5.40, 9.25, 6.52, 7.27, *8.27, then every 30 minutes until 10.27, 10.55 p. m.	
	Tyngsboro, 6.00, 6.55, 7.27 a. m. *8.07, then every 40 minutes until 12.47, 1.17, then every 30 minutes until 10.47 p. m. Return 5.40, 6.20, 6.57 a. m., then every 40 minutes unti 12.57, then 1.32, then every 30 minutes until 10.32.	
	No. Chelmsford, 6.00, 6.30, 6.55, 7.07, *8.07, then every 20 minutes until 12.47, 1.02, then every 15 minutes until 10.47. Return 5.55, 6.37, 6.57, then every 20 minutes until 1.17, 1.32, then every 15 minutes until 10.47.	
	Pawtucketville, 5.40, 6.00, 6.16, 6.36, 6.52, *7.00 then 12, 22 and 52 minutes past the hour until 10.52 p. m., then 11.15. Return 5.58, 6.18, 6.34, 6.54, 7.12, *7.15, then 12, 32 and 52 minutes past the hour until 10.52 p. m.	
Medford	North Woburn, via Winchester and Woburn, leave Medford 6.30, 9.00 a. m., then every 30 minutes until 10.00 p. m. Return leave North Woburn 5.45 a. m., *8.15, then every 30 minutes until 9.45, ‡10.15 p.m.	

*First car Sunday.   †Saturdays only.   ‡To Winchester only.

LOWELL TO SALISBURY BEACH

Via Lawrence and Haverhill.

TRUNK LINE AND BRANCHES.

From	To	Mileage		Rate of Fare		Run'g Time	
		Between Stations.	From Lowell.	Between Stations.	From Lowell.	Between Stations.	From Lowell.
						Hr Min	Hr Min
Lowell,	Lawrence,			10		15	1 00
Lawrence,	Andover,	4		5		30	
	No. Andover,	4		5		30	
	Methuen,	2		5		20	
	Haverhill,	9½	19½	10	25	1 00	2 00
Haverhill,	Ward Hill,	3		5		18	
	Groveland,	3½		5		22	
	So. Groveland, Georgetown,	5½		10		40	
	West Newbury,	6½		10		37	
	Newburyport,	13		20		1 08	
	Plum Island,	17		25		1 45	
	Merrimac,	6	25½	10	35	45	2 45
Merrimac,	Newburyport,	9		20		1 00	
	*Plum Island,	12		25		1 30	
	*Newbury,	12		25		1 55	
	Amesbury,	4½	30	10	45	30	3 15
Amesbury,	Newburyport,	5		10		35	
	*Newbury,	9		15		1 00	
	*Plum Island,	8		15		1 15	
	†Hamp'n Falls.	8		10		40	
Salisbury,	Salisbury,	4	34	5	50	30	3 45
	Newburyport,	2		5		15	
	*Newbury,	4		5		30	
	*Plum Island,	7		15		1 00	
	Seabrook,	3½		5		17	
	Hampton Falls	5½		10		27	
	Hampton,	8		10		40	
	Hamp'n Beach	10½		15		52	
	Exeter,	15		20		1 15	
	Salisbury Beach,	1⅓	36⅓	5	55	15	4 00

For Detail Time Table see pages 46 and 47

*Change cars at Newburyport.

†This line will be in operation about June 15, running through to Hampton, Hampton Beach and Exeter, N. H.

TIME - TABLE.

Lowell to Salisbury Beach.

CARS LEAVE	FOR	AT
Lowell	Lawrence, 5.25, 6.15, 7.00, then every 30 minutes until 10.30 p. m., *7.00. Return 5.25, 6.15, 7.00, then every 30 minutes until 10.30, *7.00.	
Lawrence	Andover, 5.50, 6.40, 7.15, a. m., then every 30 minutes until 11.45, 11.55, then every 20 minutes until 10.35, p. m. *8.45. Return at 5.45, then from Seminary Hill, 6.20, 7.15, then every 30 minutes until 12.15, 12.30, 12.50, 1.10, 1.30, then every 20 minutes until 10.30 p. m. *9.15.	
	No. Andover, 5.50 a. m., then every 20 minutes until 10.30 p. m., *8.30. Return 5.45, 6.20, then every 20 minutes until 10.00 p. m., *9.00.	
	Methuen, 5.30 a. m., then every 20 minutes until 11.30, then every 10 minutes until 8.50 p. m., then every 20 minutes until 10.35, *6.50. Return 20 minutes later.	
	Haverhill, 6.00, 7.00, then every 30 minutes until 10.30, *7.00. Return 6.00, 7.00, then every 30 minutes until 10.30, *7.00.	
Haverhill	Ward Hill, 6.10, 6.42, 7.17, then every 30 minutes until 10.17, *7.47. Return 6.30, 7.05, then every 30 minutes until 10.35, *8.05.	
	So. Groveland, 6.30, then every 30 minutes until 10.30, *8.30. Return 6.15 a. m., then every 30 minutes until 10.15, *8.15.	
	Georgetown, 6.30, then every 30 minutes until 10.30, *8.30, Return 6.00, then every 30 minutes until 10.00, *8.00.	
	Groveland Bridge, Groveland, 5.08, 6.00, 6.08, 6.45, 7.08, then every 30 minutes until 10.38, *7.08, 7.00.	
	West Newbury, 5.08, 6.08, then hourly until 12.08, then every 30 minutes until 10.38, *7.08. Return 6.15 from Town Hall West Newbury, then hourly until 1.15, then every 30 minutes until 11.15, *8.15.	
	Newburyport, via Peoples line, 5.08, then hourly until 12.08 then every 30 minutes until 10.08 p. m., *7.08. Return 5.45, then hourly until 12.45, then every 30 minutes until 10.45 *7.45.	
	Newburyport, via (H. & A.) 7.00 a. m., then every 30 minutes until 8.30 p. m., *8.00. Return same time.	
	Merrimac, 7.00 a. m., then every 30 minutes until 11.00 p. m., *800. Return 6.15, and then every 30 minutes until 10.15 p. m., *7.15.	
Merrimac	Newburyport, 6.15, then every 30 minutes until 9.15, *7.15. Return 7.00, then every 30 minutes until 10.30, *8.00.	
	Amesbury, 6.15, then every 30 minutes until 9.45 p. m., *7.15. Return 30 minutes later.	
Amesbury	Newburyport, 6.45 then every 30 minutes until 9.45 p. m. *7.45. Return 7.00, then every 30 minutes until 10.30 p. m. *8.00.	
	Salisbury, 6.45, then every 30 minutes until 10.15 p. m., *7.45. Return 7.10, 7.40, then every 30 minutes until 10.40, *8.10.	

*First car Sunday.

TIME - TABLE.

Lowell to Salisbury Beach—Continued.

CARS LEAVE	FOR	AT
Amesbury..........	Hampton Beach and Exeter, N. H., via Salisbury, Seabrook, Hampton Falls and Hampton on the hour and half hour. Return, leave Hampton and Exeter at the same time.	
Salisbury	Newburyport, 6.30, 7.10, then every thirty minutes until 10.10, *7.40. Return 7.00, 7.30, *8.00, then every 30 minutes until 10.30.	
	Salisbury Beach, 5.50, 6.30, 7.10, then every 30 minutes until 9.40, *7.40. Return 6.00, 6.45, 7.30, then every 30 minutes until 10.00, *8.00.	
Newburyport	Plum Island, every 30 minutes after July 1st.	
	Newbury, Old Town, every 30 minutes.	
	Hampton Beach and Exeter, N. H., via Salisbury, Seabrook, Hampton Falls and Hampton on the hour and half hour. Return leave Hampton Beach and Exeter for Newbury port at the same time.	

*First car Sunday.   †This line will be in operation about June 1st.

A "Hurry Up" Call for Power
COMES OFTEN ON
NEW ENGLAND STREET RAILWAYS.

New River Steam Coal
Is a Quick and Economical Steam Producer.

The Boston Elevated Railroad Co. use annually 100,000 Tons
Of New River Steam Coal. New River is the favorite fuel among Electric Light and Power Stations in New England.

C. H. SPRAGUE & SON,

LOCAL AGENTS IN
ALL LARGE CITIES
OF NEW ENGLAND.

70 KILBY ST., BOSTON.
NEW ENGLAND AGENTS.

BOSTON TO NEWPORT, R. I.

Via Brockton, Taunton and Fall River.

TRUNK-LINE AND BRANCHES

From	To.	Mileage.		Rate of Fare		Run'g Time	
		Between Stations.	From Boston.	Between Stations.	From Boston.	Between Stations.	From Boston.
						Hr Min	Hr Min
Boston,	Neponset,		5½		5		43
*Neponset,	Squantum,	4		5		20	
	Atlantic,	½	6	5	10	4	47
Atlantic,	Wollaston,	1	7	5	10	8	55
Wollaston,	Quincy,	1¼	8¼	5	10	8	1 03
Quincy,	Hough's Neck,	5			5		20
	So. Quincy,	1			5		07
	West Quincy,	2½			5		20
	East Milton,	3½			5		25
	§Mattapan,						
	§Mil'n Lwr. Mls						
	Braintree,	2	10¼	5	13	14	1 17
†Braintree,	East Braintree,	1		5		15	
	Weym'th Ld'g	2		5		12	
	South Braintree,	2	12¼	5	13	7	1 24
South Braintree,	Randolph,	2		5		25	
	Avon,	7¼		10		40	
	Holbrook,	3	16¼	5	18	21	1 45
Holbrook,	Brookville,	2½	18¾	5	23	17	2 02
Brookville,	Montello,	1½	20¼	5	28	10	2 12
Montello,	Brockton,	2	22¼	5	28	14	2 26
Brockton,	Brockton Ht's.	2½		5		20	
	Stoughton,	5¼		10		35	
	Avon,	4		5		30	
	Randolph,	6½		10		45	
	E. Bridgewater	6		10		45	
	Abington,	5		10		30	
	Whitman,	6		5		45	
	‡No. Easton,	4¾		10		30	
	South Easton,	6		10		30	
	No. Raynham,	11		15		45	
	Prattville,	12		15		50	
	Taunton,	15⅔		20		1 00	

For detail Time Tables see pages 51, 52 and 53.

*Through cars to Hingham & Nantasket Beach. †Through cars to Bridgewater via South Weymouth, Rockland, Abington & Whitman. ‡This line connects with cars for Mansfield, Norton, etc. §This line will be in operation about June 20, 1899.

BOSTON TO NEWPORT, R. I.

Via Brockton, Taunton and Fall River.

Continued.

TRUNK-LINE AND BRANCHES.

From	To	Mileage. Between Stations.	Mileage. From Boston.	Rate of Fare Between Stations.	Rate of Fare From Boston.	Run'g Time Between Stations. Hr Min	Run'g Time From Boston. Hr Min
Brockton,	Campello,	1½	23¾	5	28	10	2 36
Campello,	Clifton Heights,	½	24¼	5	28	03	2 39
Clifton Heights,	W. Bridgewater	3	27¼	5	33	12	2 51
W. Bridgewater,	Bridgewater,	3½	30¾	5	38	10	3 01
Bridgewater,	Scotland,	1½	32¼	5	43	10	3 11
Scotland,	Raynham,	6	38¼	5	48	30	3 41
Raynham,	Taunton,	3½	41¾	5	53	15	3 56
Taunton,	Annawon Rock or Dighton,	5½		10		25	
	Westville,	2½		5		15	
	Rehoboth,	9		15		36	
	Seekonk,	13½		20		50	
	Providence,	17½		25		1 15	
	East Taunton,	4		30		30	
	*Lakeville,						
	*Middleborough Brittannia, Brittanniaville or Whittenton,	1½		5		15	
	Prospect Hill, Scadding Pond	2¾		5		20	
	Weir Village,	1¼		5		15	
	Sabbatia Park,	2¾		5		20	
North Dighton,	North Dighton,	4	45¾	5	58	30	4 26
Berkeley,	Berkeley,	2	47¾	5	63	10	4 36
Dighton,	Dighton,	2	49¾	5	68	10	4 46
Somerset,	Somerset,	3½	53¼	5	73	20	5 06
Pottersville,	Pottersville,	1½	54¾	5	73	5	5 11
Slades Ferry,	Slades Ferry,	2	56¾	5	73	15	5 26
Bowensville,	Bowensville,	½	57¼	5	78	03	5 29
Fall River,	Fall River,	1	58¼	5	78	07	5 36
	Border City Vil.	2⅛		5		15	
	Globe Village,	2		5		15	

For detail Time Tables see pages 51, 52, and 53.

*This line will probably be in operation about August, 1899.

BOSTON TO NEWPORT, R. I.

Via Brockton, Taunton and Fall River.
Continued.

TRUNK LINE AND BRANCHES.

From	To	Mileage. Between Stations.	Mileage. From Boston.	Rate of Fare Between Stations.	Rate of Fare From Boston.	Run'g Time Between Stations.	Run'g Time From Boston.
						Hr Min	Hr Min
Fall River.	Notre Dame } Cemetery, }	3		5		30	
	Stafford Road } Station, }	1¾		5		15	
	Oak Grove Cem	2		5		15	
	Flint Village,	2		5		10	
	Watuppa Pond } or No.Westport. }	2¾		5		17	
	Westp't Factory / or Lincoln Park,)	6¾		10		36	
	No. Dartmouth / or Smith's Mills,)	10¼		15		47	
	New Bedford,	13¾		20		1 05	
	*Orphns Home	14¾		20		1 20	
	*Lund's Cor.	18¼		20		1 40	
	*Fairhaven, } *F't Phœnix, }	20¼		20		1 25	
	*Oxford V'lge or) Riverside Cem.)	22		20		1 25	
	*Howland Vil.	22		20		1 25	
	*Mt. Pleasant,	22		20		1 25	
	Tiverton,	2¾	61	10	88	15	5 51
Tiverton,	Portsmouth,	4	65	5	93	25	6 16
Portsmouth,	Middletown,	7½	72½	5	98	40	6 56
Middletown,	Newport, R. I.	3¼	75¾	5	1 03	15	7 11

For detail Time Tables see pages 51, 52 and 53.

* To reach these points from Fall River it is necessary to change cars at New Bedford where a free transfer is issued.

TIME - TABLE.

Boston to Newport, R. I.

CARS LEAVE	FOR	AT
Boston,..........	Neponset, about every 15 minutes.	
Neponset.	Squantum at 6.30, then hourly until 8.30 p. m. Return 30 minutes later.	
	Quincy, via Atlantic and Wollaston at 6.20, 6.35, 6.55, then every 15 minutes until 11.35. Return 6.00, 6.15, 6.30, then every 15 minutes until 11.15 p. m.	
Quincy	East Weymouth, via North Weymouth, 5.45, 6.20, then every 30 minutes until 10.50. Return 6.00, then every 30 minutes until 11.30 p. m.	
	Weymouth Landing, 5.30, 6.20, then hourly until 12.20 p. m., then 12.50, then hourly until 10.50. Return 5.50, then hourly until 12.50 p. m., then 1.20 and hourly until 11.20 p. m.	
	East Milton, 5.55, 6.25, then 5 minutes of, and 25 minutes past the hour, until 9.25, then 10.50 a. m. Return 30 minutes later.	
	Hough's Neck, 6.20, then hourly until 11.20 a. m., then 12.50 p. m., then hourly until 9.50, then hourly until 10.45, then 1.20 p. m., and hourly until 9.20 p. m.	
	South Quincy, 5.55, 6.40, 6.55, 7.25, then every 30 minutes until 9.50 p. m., then 10.50 p. m. Return 6.40, 7.10, then every 30 minutes until 9.40 p. m., 10.40 and 11.40 p. m.	
	West Quincy, same as South Quincy Return 6.35, 7.05, then every 30 minutes until 9.35 p. m., then 10.35 and 11.35.	
	Braintree, 6.10, 6.40, then every 30 minutes until 10.10 p. m. Return 6.25, 6.55, then every 30 minutes until 11.25.	
Braintree	South Braintree, at 6.25, 6.55, then every 30 minutes until 10.25 p. m. Return 6.15, 6.45, then every 30 minutes until 11.15 p. m.	
South Braintree	Holbrook, 5.35, 6.05, then every 30 minutes until 10.35 p. m. Return 5.55, 6.25, then every 30 minutes until 10.55 p. m.	
	Randolph, and Avon or Highland Park.	
Holbrook.	South Weymouth.	
	Brockton via Brookville and Montello, 6.05, 6.15, 6.25, 6.55, 7.25, *7.55, then every 30 minutes until 10.25 p. m. Return 5.20, 5.30, 5.55, 6.25, *7.25, then every 30 minutes until 9.55 p. m.	
Brockton..	Brockton Heights and Stoughton, 5.30, 5.45, *6.45, then every 30 minutes until 10.45 p. m. Return 6.00, 6.15, 6.45, *7.15, then every 30 minutes until 11.15 p. m.	
	Randolph, 5.15, 5.35, 6.15, 6.45 a. m., *7.15, then every 30 minutes until 9.45 p. m. Return 6.00, 6.10, 6.20, 7.00, *8.00, then every 30 minutes until 10.30 p. m.	
	Highland Park, about every 10 minutes, *7.05. Return, first car, 6.07, *7.17, last car, 11.57 p. m.	
	Avon, 5.15, 5.25, 5.35, 5.38, 5.40, 6.15, 6.35, 6.45, 7.05, *7.15, and at least every 30 minutes until 10.45 p. m.	

*Indicates first car on Sunday.
Cars leaving Neponset 20 minutes past the hour go via Norolfk Downs. Cars leaving Quincy on the even hour go via Norfolk Downs.

TIME-TABLE.

Boston to Newport, R. I.—Continued.

CARS LEAVE	FOR	AT
Brockton...........	†East Bridgewater, 6.40, 7.00, 7.40 *8.30, then hourly until 10.30 p. m. Return 6.00 and *8.00, then every 30 minutes until 10.00 p. m.
	Abington, 6.00, *7.30, then every 30 minutes until 10.30 p. m. Return same time.
	Whitman, 6.00, 6.15, 6.30 a. m., *7.30, then every 30 minutes until 10.30 p. m. Return 6.00, 6.30, *7.15, then every 30 minutes until 10.30 p. m.
	North Easton, 5.45 a. m., *6.45, then every 30 minutes until 10.45 p. m. Return 30 minutes later.
	Taunton, via South Easton, North Raynham and Prattville, 6.00 a. m., then every 30 minutes until 9.00 p. m. *6.00. Return leave Taunton 6.00 a. m., then every 30 miuutes until 10.30 p. m., *7.00.
	Campbello, every 10 minutes.
	†Taunton, via West Bridgewater, Scotland and Raynham, 6.40 a. m., then every 30 minutes until 9.30 p. m., 10.00, 10.30, 11.00, 11.30 to West Bridgewater. Return leave Taunton 6 50 a. m., then every 30 minutes until 10.20 p. m., 10.50. (11.20, 11.50 to Lake Neppconickit only.)
Taunton	Providence, via Rehoboth and Seekonk, 6.40 a. m., then every 30 minutes until 9.50 p. m. Return leave Providence, 7.05 a. m., then hourly until 9.05 p. m.
	Fall River, via Berkeley, Dighton and Somerset, 5.15, 6.07, a.m., then hourly until 1.07, then every 30 minutes until 9.07 p. m. Return leave Fall River 6.20, 7.30 a. m., then hourly until 1.30, then every 30 minutes until 9.30 p. m.
	East Taunton, 6.10, 6.15, 7.00, *8.30 then every 30 minutes until 10.30 p. m. Return 5.45, 6.30 a. m. *8.00, then every 30 minutes until 10.00 p. m
	Sabbatia Park, 7.00, then every 15 minutes until 11 p. m. Return 15 minutes later.
	Whittenton, 5.30, *7.45, then every 30 minutes until 11.00.
	Brittanniaville, 5.45 a. m., *7.45, then every 30 minutes until 10.30 p. m. Return 15 minutes earlier.
‡Fall River..........	New Bedford, via North Dartmouth and Westport, 5.50, 6.50, 7.50 a. m., *8.20, then every 30 minutes until 9.50 p. m., then 10.40. Return leave New Bedford 5.45, 7.05, 7.35 a. m., then every 30 minutes until 10.35 p. m., *8.05.
	Newport, R. I., via Tiverton, Portsmouth and Middletown, 6.15, 6.45 a. m., *7.45, then every 30 minutes until 9.15 p. m. Return 7.15, 8.15, *8.15 a. m., then every 30 minutes until 9.15 p. m.
	Border City Village, 5.55, 6.10, then every 10 minutes until 9.30, then every 15 minutes until 11.30. Return 5.30, then every 10 minutes until 9.45, then every 15 minutes until 10.45.

* Indicates first car on Sunday.   † Take car at railroad station, Brockton.
‡ All cars leave City Hall.

TIME-TABLE.

Boston to Newport, R. I.—Continued.

Cars Leave	For	At
Fall River..........	Notre Dame Cemetery, 5.55, 6.30, then every 30 minutes until 12.00, then every 15 minutes until 8.00, then every 30 minutes until 11.00.	
†**New Bedford**	Oak Grove Cemetery, 5.25, 5.45, 5.55, 6.15, then every 15 minutes until 11.00 p. m. Return 15 minutes later.	
	Oak Grove Cemetery.	
	Brooklawn Park and Lund's Corner, on the hour and every 10 minutes. Return 5 minutes later.	
	Marine Park, on the hour and every 10 minutes. Return 5 mintues later.	
	Mount Pleasant, 5 minutes past the hour and every 15 minutes. Return same time.	
	Rockdale Ave. and Dartmouth St., 5 minutes past the hour and every 15 minutes. Return same time.	
	Padanaram, 20 minutes past the hour and every 30 minutes. Return same time.	
	Kempton St. & Buttonwood Park, 10 minutes past the hour and every 15 minutes. Return same time.	
	Summer Street, 5 minutes past the hour and every 20 minutes. Return 10 minutes later.	
	Fairhaven and Fort Phœnix, 5 minutes past the hour and every 15 minutes. Return 8 minutes later.	
	Oxford and Riverside Cemetery. On arrival of car from New Bedford at 15 minutes past the hour and every 15 minutes. Return 7 minutes past the hour and every 15 minutes.	

BOSTON TO BROCKTON

Via Quincy, Hingham and Rockland.

TRUNK LINE AND BRANCHES.

From	To.	Mileage Between Stations.	Mileage From Boston.	Rate of Fare Between Stations.	Rate of Fare From Boston.	Run'g Time Between Stations. Hr Min	Run'g Time From Boston. Hr Min
Boston,	Neponset,		5½		5		43
*Neponset,	Quincy,	2¾	8¼	5	10	20	1 03
Quincy,	Quincy Point,	1¼	9½	5	13	09	1 12
Quincy Point,	No. Weymouth,	2	11½	5	13	14	1 26
No. Weymouth,	Fort Point,	1		5		07	
	Bradley's } Fertilizer, }	1		5		10	
	Hingham,	3	14½	5	18	20	1 46
Hingham,	Nantasket,	3		5		15	
	East Weymouth,	3		5		15	
	Braintree,	5		10		40	
	So. Hingham,	2	16½	5	23	15	2 01
So. Hingham,	No. Hanover,	3	19½	5	28	15	2 16
†No. Hanover,	Rockland,	5	24½	5	28	15	2 31
Rockland,	No. Abington,	2		5		10	
	Abington via } No. Abington, }	4		5		20	
	Whitman via } No. Abington, }	6		5		30	
	Abington,	2	26¼	5	33	10	2 41
Abington,	Brockton,	4	30¼	5	38	20	3 01

For Detail Time-Table see Page 56.

* A through line of cars are run from Neponset to Nantasket Beach without change.
† Change cars for Assinippi.

BOSTON TO BRIDGEWATER.

Via Quincy, East Weymouth, Rockland and Whitman.

TRUNK LINE AND BRANCHES.

From	To	Mileage Between Stations	Mileage From Boston	Rate of Fare Between Stations	Rate of Fare From Boston	Run'g Time Between Stations (Hr Min)	Run'g Time From Boston (Hr Min)
Boston,	Neponset,		5½		5		43
Neponset,	Quincy,	2¾	8¼	5	10	20	1 03
Quincy,	Quincy Point,	1¼	9½	5	13	9	1 12
Quincy Point,	No. Weymouth,	2	11½	5	13	14	1 26
No. Weymouth,	E. Weymouth,	2½	14	5	18	20	1 46
E. Weymouth,	Lovells Corner,	1	15	5	23	7	1 53
Lovells Corner,	So. Weymouth,	2½	17½	5	23	20	2 13
So. Weymouth,	Rockland,	4½	22	5	28	25	2 38
*Rockland,	Whitman,	4	26½	5	33	25	3 03
Whitman,	E. Bridgewater,	3½	30	5	38	15	3 18
E. Bridgewater,	Bridgewater,	3½	33½	5	43	15	3 33
Bridgewater,	†Middleborough,		5		5		20
	†Lakeville,		10		10		45
	†Freetown,		14		15		1 00
	†New Bedford,		20¼		20		1 15
	Lund's Corner,		26¾		25		1 30
	Fairhaven,		30½		30		2 00

*Change for Assinippi.   †This line will be in operation about July 10th.

For Detail Time Table see page 56.

TIME-TABLE.

Boston to Brockton and Bridgewater, via Hingham, So. Weymouth, and Rockland.

CARS LEAVE	FOR	AT
Brockton............	Nantasket Beach via Abington, Rockland and Hingham at 6.30 a. m., then every 30 minutes until 8.oo p. m. Abington, 20 minutes later. Rockland, 30 minutes later.	
Nantasket Beach ...	Brockton via Hingham, Rockland and Abington at 7.oo a. m. then every 30 minutes until 9.30 p. m. Hingham, 20 minutes later. Rockland, one hour later. Abington, one hour 10 minutes later.	
Neponset............	Nantasket Beach via Hingham at 7.oo a. m., then every 30 minutes until 8.oo p. m. Hingham, one hour later.	
Nantasket Beach ...	Neponset, 7.oo a. m., then every 30 minutes until 9.30 p. m. Hingham, 25 minutes later.	
Braintree	Bridgewater via Weymouth, So. Weymouth, Rockland, Abington and Whitman at 6.30 a. m., then every 30 minutes until 7.30 p. m. Weymouth, 10 minutes later. So. Weymouth, 30 minutes later. Rockland, 45 minutes later. Whitman, one hour later.	
Bridgewater	Braintree via Whitman, Rockland, So. Weymouth and Weymouth at 6.30 a. m., then every 30 minutes until 7.30 p. m. Whitman, 45 minutes later. Rockland, one hour later. So. Weymouth, one hour 20 minutes later. Weymouth, one hour 40 minutes later.	
Rockland............	Whitman via No. Abington at 6.oo a. m., then every 30 minutes until 10.oo p. m. No. Abington, 10 minutes later.	
Whitman	Rockland, 6.30 a. m., then every 30 minutes until 10.oo p. m. No. Abington, 20 minutes later.	
Hingham............	Nantasket Beach, 6.30 a. m., and every 30 minutes until 9.30 p.m. Return at 6.55, 7.30 a. m., then every 30 minutes until 9.00 a. m., then every 15 minutes until 9.oo p. m. Braintree, 6.15 a. m., then every 30 minutes until 10.15 p. m. Return at 7.oo a. m., then every 30 minutes until 9.30 p. m.	
So. Weymouth	E. Weymouth, 6.45, then every 30 minutes until 9.15 p. m., Return 7.15 a. m., then every 30 minutes until 9.45 p. m.	

BOSTON TO DEDHAM.

Via Hyde Park.

TRUNK LINE AND BRANCHES.

From	To	Mileage Between Stations.	Mileage From Boston.	Rate of Fare Between Stations.	Rate of Fare From Boston.	Run'g Time Between Stations. Hr Min	Run'g Time From Boston. Hr Min
Boston,	Forest Hills,		4½		5		40
Forest Hills,	Mount Hope,	1	5½	5	10	06	46
Mount Hope,	Clarendon Hills,	1½	7	5	10	05	51
Clarendon Hills,	Hazelwood,	½	7½	5	10	03	54
Hazelwood,	Hyde Park,	½	8	5	10	05	59
•Hyde Park,	Readville,	1		5		07	
	†Mattapan,	2		5		12	
	†Milt. Low. Falls	3½				26	
	East Dedham,						
East Dedham,	Dedham,		11	5	10		1 24

For detail Time Table see pages 59 and 60.

*Free transfers to Readville, Mattapan and Milton Lower Mills and visa versa.

†A line will be in operation about June 20, running from these points to Quincy and Randolph.

BOSTON TO PROVIDENCE

Via Dedham, Walpole and Mansfield.

TRUNK-LINE AND BRANCHES.

From	To	Mileage Between Stations	Mileage From Boston	Rate of Fare Between Stations	Rate of Fare From Boston	Run'g Time Between Stations	Run'g Time From Boston
Boston,	Forest Hills,		4½		5		40
Forest Hills,	Central,	2		5		11	
	Highland,	2½		5		18	
	West Roxbury,	3		5		20	
	Spring Street,	3¾		5		22	
	Germantown,	4¾		5		25	
	East Dedham,	5½		5		30	
	Oakdale,	6		5		35	
	*Needham,	8		10		45	
	Roslindale,	1¼	5¾	5	10	08	48
Roslindale,	Germantown,	2¼	8¼	5	10	15	1 03
Germatown,	Dedham,	1	9¼	5	10	07	1 10
Dedham,	Westwood,	5		5		20	
	Medfield,	10		10		40	
	Norwood,	4	13¼	5	15	36	1 46
Norwood,	East Walpole,	2	15¼	5	15	11	1 57
	Walpole,	4½	17¾	5	20	20	2 17
Walpole,	East Walpole,	3		5		15	
	South Walpole,	2	19¾	5	25	10	2 27
South Walpole,	North Foxboro,	2½	22¼	5	25	15	2 42
North Foxboro,	Foxboro,	2	24¼	5	30	10	2 52
Foxboro,	Wrentham,	2		5		10	
	Mansfield,	4	28¼	5	30	20	3 12
Mansfield,	Furnace Village	6¼		10		30	
	North Easton,	10½		15		45	
	Brockton,	15		25		1 15	
	Norton,	5½	33¾	10	40	25	3 37
Norton,	Norton Furnace	4		5		15	
	Taunton,	8½		10		35	
	Chartley,	2¼		5		15	
Chartley,	Attleboro,	5¾	39½	10	50	25	4 02
Attleboro,	North Attleboro	4		5		30	
	Plainville,	6		10		45	
	Dodgeville,	2½	44	5	55	10	4 12
Dodgeville,	Lebanon Mills,	4	48	5	60	20	4 32
Lebanon Mills,	Pawtucket,	1½	49½	5	60	10	4 42
Pawtucket,	Providence,	4	53½	5	65	30	5 12

For detail Time Tables see pages 59 and 60.

*This line will be in operation about July 1st, 1890.

TIME-TABLE.

Hyde Park, Dedham, Mansfield, Providence and Branches.

CARS LEAVE	FOR	AT
Forest Hills.........	Dedham via Clarendon Hill and Hyde Park, 6.00 a. m., then every 15 minutes until 7.45 p. m., then every 30 minutes until 11.45 p. m., then 12.10. Return at 5.40, 6.00, 6.30 a. m., then every 15 minutes until 8.00 p. m., then every 30 minutes until 11.30 p. m.	
	Readville via Clarendon Hill and Hyde Park, 6.00 a. m., then every 30 minutes until 10.30 p. m. Return 6.30, then every 30 minutes until 11.00 p. m.	
	Oakdale via Roslindale, Highland, Spring St., and West Roxbury at 5.45 a. m., then every 30 minutes until 12.15 p.m., 12.55, then every 30 minutes until 11.25 p. m., then 12.05. Return at 5.25 a. m., then every 30 minutes until 12.25, 1.05 p. m., then every 30 minutes until 11.35 p. m.	
	¹Charles River (Spring St.) via Roslindale, Central, Highland and West Roxbury, 5.45 a. m., then every 30 minutes until 11.15 p. m. Return 6.10 a. m., then every 30 minutes until 11.40 p. m.	
	Westwood Park and E. Walpole, via Roslindale, Germantown and Dedham, 5.30 a. m., then every 30 minutes until 1.30, then every 15 minutes until 8.30, then every 30 minutes until 11.30 p. m., *7.00.	
Dedham	Westwood and Medfield, 6.00 a. m., then every 30 minutes until 11.00 p. m., then 11.40. Return at 5.45 a. m., then every 30 minutes until 10.45 p. m.	
	Mattapan & Milton Lower Mills, 6.45 a. m., then every 30 minutes until 7.45 p. m. Return at 6.00 a. m., then every 30 minutes until 7.30 p. m.	
	Forest Hills, 5.30 p. m., then every 30 minutes until 1.30 p. m., then every 15 minutes until 8.30, then every 30 minutes until 11.30 p. m.	
	East Walpole via Westwood Park and Norwood at 6.00 a. m., then every 30 minutes until 10.30 p. m.	
Hyde Park	‡Mattapan and Milton Lower Mills, 5.37 a. m., then every 30 minutes until 8.07 p. m., 8.21, then every 30 minutes until 10.21 p. m., then 11.07 p. m. Return at 6.00 a. m., then every 30 minutes until 11.30 p. m.	
Norwood	Walpole, Foxboro and Mansfield on the hour and half-hour.	
Mansfield	Taunton via Norton at 5.30, then hourly until 10.30 p. m. Return 6.15 a. m., then hourly until 10.15 p. m.	
	North Easton, 15 minutes before the hour and then hourly. Return same time.	
Norton	Attleboro, 5.30 a. m., then hourly until 11.30 p. m.	
	Mansfield, 5.00 a. m., then hourly until 11.00 p. m.	
	Taunton, at 5.00 a. m., then every 30 minutes until 11.00 p. m.	

† The line from Charles River to Needham will be in operation about July 1st.

‡ A line will be in operation about June 20th running from these points to East Milton there connecting with the Quincy & Boston, and to Randolph connecting with the Brockton Street Railway.

TIME-TABLE.

Hyde Park, Dedham, Mansfield, Providence and Branches — Continued.

CARS LEAVE	FOR AT
Taunton	Attleboro, 5.45 a. m., then hourly until 10.45 p. m.
No. Attleboro	Pawtucket via So. Attleboro, 5.20 a. m., then every 30 minutes until 10.50 p. m. Return 6.05 a. m., then every 30 minutes until 11.35 p. m.
Attleboro	Pawtucket and Providence, via Dodgeville and Lebanon Mills, 5.20 a. m., then every 30 minutes until 12.05 midnight. Return at 5.20 a. m., then every 30 minutes until 11.20 p. m.
	Plainville via No. Attleboro at 5.35 a. m., then every 30 minutes until 11.15 p. m. Return at 6.10, 6.40, 7.20, 8.00 a. m., then every 30 minutes until 12.00 midnight.

Picturesque
BUILDING LOTS
AT
Oakhurst.
(OAKHURST MEANING OAK HOME.)

BRANCH LINES FROM PROVIDENCE.

From	To	Mileage.	Rate of Fare.	Running Time.	
				Hrs.	Min.
Providence,	Arlington,	2½	5		22
	Attleboro,	12	15		40
	Auburn,	5½	5		35
	Cranson,	2½	5		20
	Centredale,	5	10		30
	Dodgeville,	9	5		50
	Dyerville,	3	5		25
	Edgewood,	4	5		23
	East Providence,	2¾	5		12
	E. Providence Cen.	6 1-6	5		48
	Fox Point,	1 1-6	10		15
	Hebronville,	8	7		45
	Lakewood,	5¾	5		40
	Lonsdale Station,	3¼	5		25
	Merino,	3	5		25
	Manton,	4¾	5		38
	Meshanticut Park,	5½	5		39
	Mount Pleasant,	2½	5		24
	N. Attleboro,	12	15	1	30
	N. Attleboro via Attleboro, }	16½	20	1	30
	Old Town,	9	10		50
	Olneyville,	2	5		20
	Pawtucket,	4	5		25
	Plainville,	14	20	1	15
	Pawtuxet,	4¾	5		32
	Phillipsdale	5¾	5		48
	Riverside,	7⅓	10		50
	Riverpoint,	13	15		70
	Roger Williams Prk	4¾	5		25
	Rocky Hill,	3¾	5		30
	South Attleboro,	8	10		45
	Saylesville,	2½	5		18
	Thornton,	4¾	5		39
	Valley Falls,	2	5		16
	Wanskuck,	3	5		28
	Washington Park,	3⅓	5		27

Around Boston by Trolley.

IN no better way can one see the sights of Boston than by a trip on the electric cars of the Boston Elevated Railway Company. For the small sum of ten cents it is possible to visit any part of the city and many of the suburbs. Some of the rides are long, and by making changes at the free transfer stations of the company, at Park street in the Subway, at Dudley Street, Roxbury Crossing, Broadway in South Boston, Harvard Square and Craigie Bridge in Cambridge or Sullivan Square in Charlestown, a great variety of trips is possible for this small sum. The electric car rides are becoming more popular every year, as a greater number of people come to know the pleasure of travelling in this fashion, while trolley trips by parties on special cars, form a delightful method of combining amusement and instruction. It is impossible, in the limits of a few pages, to give more than a brief outline of what may be seen on these trolley trips on the cars of the Boston Elevated Railway. Reference to the tables on Page 22 and following, will show where one may take a car for any point in the city. For the benefit of those who wish to make these cheapest of all excursions, or who wish to show visiting friends the city, the following round trips, covering all the principal lines in the city, have been sketched.

THROUGH BROOKLINE. Take a brown Reservoir car in the Subway, emerging at the Public Garden, passing Arlington street church on the right; then on Boylston street, past the Boston Museum of Natural History, and the Massachusetts Institute of Technology on the right; on the left, opposite, are the Boston Y. M. C. A. building and Hotel Brunswick. Entering Copley Square, Trinity Church, the Museum of Fine Arts and the Public Library are on the left, and the New Old South Church is opposite on

BOSTON PUBLIC GARDENS.

the right. At Exeter street, cars pass the Harvard Medical School on the left. Turning into Massachusetts avenue, the Fenway is seen on the left. At Commonwealth avenue, the view on the right is toward Beacon Hill, Public Garden and the Soldiers' Monument on the Common; on the left are the Lief Erickson statue and the Fens. At Beacon street, as the car turns, Harvard Bridge is on the right. On Beacon street, cars pass the Fens on the left, cross Commonwealth avenue, and leave Charles River Basin on the

New Old South Church.

Buildings in
Copley Sq.
Boston.

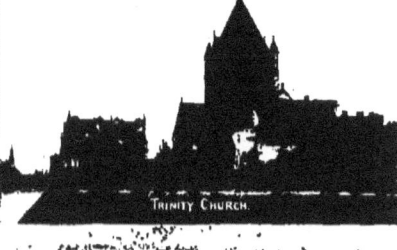

Trinity Church.

right. The ride out Beacon street is between fine houses of many of Boston's wealthiest business men, to Coolidge Corner. From here cars run over Corey Hill, rising on the right, with a fine view of Brookline on the left, passing the residences of Thomas W. Lawson and Eben D. Jordan on the right, and soon after, Beaconsfield Terrace apartment houses on the left, before reaching Reservoir station. The Reservoir is a minute's walk, ahead. Cars run up to the Newton line, to connect with Commonwealth Avenue cars. Returning, a blue car marked Huntington avenue is taken, turning off at Washington street to the right, going through Brookline Village, past the Town Hall, crossing the Fenway, passing the House of the Good Shepherd on the left, then the circus grounds and on the right the Chutes. At Gainsborough Street the Children's Hospital is on the left, and after crossing Massachusetts avenue, the Exposition building of the Massachusetts Charitable Mechanics' Association is passed. Then the car runs through Copley Square, returning to the Subway.

NEWTON, RETURNING VIA MT. AUBURN. The Newton Commonwealth avenue car from the Subway goes over the same route as the Brookline car to Commonwealth avenue, then along that, with the Charles River on the right and the Speedway on the left. At Babcock street the Allston Golf Club grounds are on the right. Passing Brighton with the old drovers' hotel on the right, the cars enter Nonantum Square, Newton. Here a change is made to a Watertown car for Bowdoin Square. The Charles River is crossed before entering Watertown. Then the car runs on Mount Auburn street, past

Mount Auburn Cemetery. Entering Cambridge after leaving the cemetery, Elmwood, James Russell Lowell's old home, is on the left, and after passing the Cambridge City Hospital on the right, Longfellow Park, the poet's old home and Washington's headquarters, are on the left. Entering Harvard Square the Harvard College buildings are on the left. Passing the Cambridge City Hall on the left, the car runs through the manufacturing district and crosses the Charles River by West Boston Bridge, with Harvard Bridge on the right and Craigie Bridge on the left. At the end of the Bridge, the Charles Street Jail is on the left. Passing through the old West End of Boston, the terminus is at Bowdoin Square, near the Scollay Square entrance of the Subway.

HARVARD COLLEGE. Taking any Harvard Square car in the Subway, the ride is as described to Beacon street and Massachusetts avenue, where Harvard Bridge is crossed. Running through the manufacturing part of Cambridge, Charles River Park is on the left, and then through the business part of the city, past the Cambridge City Hall on the right, and college dormitories, the car enters Harvard Square. Entering the grounds on the West, Massachusetts Hall, built in 1718, is on the left and Harvard Hall, built in 1765, on the right. Turning to the right, one passes Matthews' Hall and comes to Dane Hall, formerly the Law School. On the corner nearest Harvard Square is the old President's House, or Wadsworth House, used by Washington and Lee as headquarters in 1775. On the north side of the quadrangle is Gore Hall, the college library. University Hall is on the east side of the quadrangle, and

east of this are Sever Hall and Thayer Hall. Behind
Thayer Hall is Appleton Chapel. On the north and
west sides of the quadrangle are Holworthy, Stoughton and Hollis Halls, used as dormitories. Between
Hollis and Stoughton is Holden Chapel. Leaving
the college yard, across Cambridge street, is the Hem-
enway Gymnasium, and east of this the Lawrence
Scientific School, northwest of which is the new Law
School building. Going down Cambridge street, is
Memorial Hall, at the west end of which is the John
Harvard statue. East of Memorial Hall is Divinity
avenue, on which is Divinity Hall, opposite which are
the Peabody Museum and the Agassiz Museum.
Going through Quincy street, the President's house
is passed, and on the corner of Quincy and Harvard
streets is the old Dana house. Opposite this is Beck
Hall, a luxurious dormitory. College Hall is on Harvard Square, and next this is the old First Parish
Church and Burying Ground. West of the Burying
Ground is Christ Church, built in 1761, and beyond,
on Garden street, is the Washington Elm, near the
Shepard Memorial Church. A short walk up Garden
street is the Botanic Garden, opposite which is the
Harvard College Observatory. Returning to Harvard Square a Scollay Square car may be taken to
return through the residence and manufacturing districts of Cambridge and across Craigie Bridge and
around past the North Station to Scollay Square.

ARLINGTON. Any Harvard Square car may
be taken from Park Street station, but an Arlington
car goes through without change. Leaving Harvard
Square, the Botanic Gardens are passed at Linnaean
Street. On both sides are memorial tablets telling of

WADSWORTH'S
OR
PRESIDENT'S HOUSE.

CRAIGIE HOUSE
HOME OF
LONGFELLOW
AND HEADQUARTERS
OF
WASHINGTON

ELMWOOD.
HOME OF
JAMES RUSSELL LOWELL

CHRIST'S CHURCH
AND GRAVEYARD.
GAMB.

the minute men's march to Concord and Lexington. Crossing Alewive Brook, Arlington is entered. Spy Pond is to the left. At Arlington Centre are the Town Hall and Soldiers' Monument on the right and the Public Library on the left. The terminus of the line is at Arlington Heights. At Arlington connection may be made for Winchester, through which one may return to Boston via Medford for fifteen cents. The direct route is to return to Harvard Square, thence to Boston by Craigie or West Boston Bridges.

MEDFORD AND MALDEN. Taking a Medford car in the Subway or at the North Station, the ride is across the Charles River and through Charlestown, at Monument street passing Bunker Hill Monument, seen on the right. From Sullivan Square in Charlestown, the route of Paul Revere's ride is followed over Winter Hill, the best residence district. Combination and Mystic Parks, with their trotting tracks, are on the right as the car descends the hill, and Tufts College is seen on the left. At Medford, the Mystic River is crossed where the first ship built in New England was launched by Governor Winthrop. At Medford Square, in front of the old Town Hall,

BUNKER HILL MONUMENT.

a change is made to a Malden car for Boston, which
is reached by a short ride through a residence
district, returning via West Everett or Broadway.
The West Everett car goes over a hill on which are
located the fine Converse estates, on opposite sides of
the street, at Belmont Street, the car running through
West Everett to Sullivan Square. On the Broadway
car the ride is through the residence district of Malden and then through the business centre, and past
the great chemical works on the right before reaching
Sullivan Square, from which the return to Boston is
over the route traversed in going to Medford.

REVERE BEACH. This great state reservation and bathing beach is reached by taking a car at
Scollay, Adams or Haymarket Subway stations. The
ride is through Charlestown, passing the Navy Yard
on the right and Bunker Hill Monument on the left,
and affording a fine view of the Upper Harbor, passing
over Chelsea Bridge, at the end of which, on the left,
is the Marine Hospital. Going through Chelsea
Square, the car passes the first Catholic Church
erected between Boston and Salem, the Fitz Public
Library, and on the left, Powder House Hill, with its
Soldiers' Hospital. Crossing the stone bridge between Chelsea and Revere, the new and handsome
Revere Town Hall is passed, and soon the car comes
to Revere Beach, where is one of the largest and finest
bathhouses in the world. The return may be made by
the same route to Chelsea, and from there to Boston
by Chelsea Ferry, with a ride down the Upper Harbor, or by East Boston and across one of the East
Boston ferries.

MARINE PARK. Taking a Broadway South Boston car at Post Office Square or at the South Station, the car runs past the great terminal and through the main business street of South Boston, over a hill on which the famous Perkins' Institution for the Blind is seen on the right, and the harbor on the left, and soon reaches Marine Park. Here a walk past the monument to Admiral Farragut and over a bridge brings one to Castle Island, with its old fortifications, and one may walk

FARRAGUT STATUE.

along the shore to the Headhouse and Marine Pier which runs far out into Dorchester Bay. Walking back to the car line, on the left is the end of the Strandway, the great boulevard to connect Marine Park with Franklin Park, and here a Bay View car may be taken for the return. The car runs along the shore of the Bay around the hill known as Dorchester Heights, fortified by Washington in the Siege of Boston. Across the Bay on the left is the City Sewage Pumping Station. The ride to Boston is across Fort Point Channel, and through another part of the business district.

NEPONSET OR MILTON. Taking a Milton Dorchester avenue car at the North or South Stations or at Post Office Square, the ride is past the new sta-

tion and straight out Dorchester avenue, through
South Boston, and with glimpses of the Bay on the
left and dwellings on both sides of the street, to Field's
Corner. From here the ride to Milton is through a
pretty residence district, while one going to Neponset
may transfer at Park Street, Dorchester, and go out
through another residence district, with some open
country, to the terminus at the Neponset River, where
connection is made with Quincy & Boston cars. Returning from Milton, at Ashmont Street, one may
walk up the left a few blocks, and take a Washington
street car, going through Old Dorchester, past the
old Congregational Church on the right, and then the
Walter Baker Sanitarium, on a hill, affording a
fine view of the harbor before running on to Grove
Hall. Then the route is down Warren street, through
the Roxbury residence district, and down Washington
Street to Dover, turning off to go into the Subway, or
running straight down through the retail district to
Franklin Street.

FRANKLIN PARK. Take any Franklin Park
car in the Subway, or any car that goes to Dudley
Street transfer station. The Franklin Park Warren
Street car goes out to Dover Street, then crosses over
to Washington, passing the Cathedral of the Holy
Cross on the left, and at Eustis Street the burying
ground where are interred Governor Dudley and John
Eliot, the Indian Apostle. Passing Dudley street, the
ride up Warren Street is past fine residences and by
the Roxbury High School on the left, and at Elm
Hill avenue past the handsome Unitarian Church on
the right. At Grove Hall is another free transfer station. The Park car passes the Consumptives' Home

on the left before coming to the Park entrance at Columbia Road. Here, for twenty-five cents, carriages may be taken for a ride around the park, passing the Refectory Building on an elevation at the left, the golf links beyond, through the Valley Gates, around the Playstead, past the Overlook Building, then near Schoolmaster Hill, where Emerson once taught, then through the beautiful Wilderness and down through Ellicottdale with its tennis courts, and

FRANKLIN PARK.

emerging at the Arborway, from which one may go back to the city by another line of cars. The carriages continue back to the starting point, however, past a chain of lakes and by the other side of the golf course and Abbottswood to the Refectory. In returning, by changing at Grove Hall or Dudley street, almost any desired part of the city may be reached for a five-cent fare. The Park offers a succession of delightful landscapes, dales, ponds, ledges and woods alternating, and the whole ride is one of the pleasantest to be had in Boston.

FOREST HILLS. Taking a Forest Hills car in the Subway or transferring to one at Dudley street, the ride beyond Dudley street is past the steep "Tommy's Rocks" on the left, the Notre Dame Academy on the right and the New England Hospital for Women and Children, and to the terminus at Forest Hills, where the entrance to Franklin Park is at the left and the Arnold Arboretum at the right. Walking up under the railroad viaduct on the right, one enters the Arborway, and following this past a part of the Arboretum, comes to Chester street. A short walk down this brings one to the Jamaica Plain car, which returns to Boston with Jamaica Pond on the left at Pond street, and after going under the railroad tracks following the viaduct on the left toward Boston.

Norumbega and About There.

MOST Bostonians who travel on the electric cars for pleasure seek some ride which combines beautiful scenery along the route with ample means for recreation at the end of the journey. In this respect the advantages offered by the trip to Norumbega Park fulfill all requiremetns. The ride to Norumbega takes one through the finest residence portions of Boston, Brookline and "The Newtons," as the dozen little villages in the city of Newton are collectively called. The frequent and rapid service on this double-tracked line, and the low cost of the trip are some of the reasons why the Norumbega journey is so popular.

The cars start from the Subway, running via the Public Garden and Copley Square and are marked "Newton Boulevard." They also bear signs announcing that they connect with the cars of the Commonwealth Avenue Street Railway Company for Norumbega Park. The route is out Beacon Street, through the Back Bay and the beautiful residence district of Brookline, as described elsewhere under "Around Boston by Trolley," to the

RESERVOIR, where the passenger keeps on up the hill to Commonwealth Avenue. The car runs past Greenwood Cemetery on the left, and as the terminus of the line is reached, at the Newton Boundary, St. John's Roman Catholic Ecclesiastical Institution is seen, off to the right. From this hill is obtained a

fine view of the handsome residences which crown Corey Hill in Brookline, back on the right, and on the left are the large distributing reservoirs of the Boston Water Works, twin lakes connected by a silver band and surrounded by beautiful shrubbery. Changing at the terminus to one of the cars of the Com-

ON THE CHARLES.

monwealth Ave. Street Railway Company, the most beautiful part of the journey through the Newtons begins. As the car climbs Waban Hill, on the left there is a splendid view of the Chestnut Hill reservoir, while on the right are the high service and low service reservoirs of the Newton Water Works. The view from Waban Hill, on a summer day, is an inspiring one. Looking backward the summits of the Brookline hills are seen, here and there a great apartment house or splendid residence rising like a castle, while in the nearer distance the Reservoir sparkles in its emerald bowl of shrubbery and lawn. Across the Reservoir is the Boston Pumping Station. Away ahead stretch the Newtons, the many villages nestling among the trees from which peep here and there slender church spires. Southward is spread out a grand panorama of hills and dales, fields and forests. Leaving the green woods on the left the car plunges down a long incline, with an exhilarating slide down the hill to Centre Street,

NEWTON CENTRE, passing the Newton Centre Athletic Grounds on the right. Continuing on through the village, still running on Commonweath Avenue boulevard, the scenery assumes less of a metropolitan aspect. The car goes across an arm of Bullough's Pond, and past Bullough's Pond Park, just beyond, a stop being made at Walnut Street to connect with the cars of the Newton & Boston Electric Railway, which run to Newtonville, Newton Upper Falls, Highlandville and Needham, the three lines last named taking one to Echo Bridge in the Hemlock Gorge Reservation, one of the finest of the smaller state parks. At the junction there is a commodious and attractive street railway waiting station. This region is in the exact centre of Newton and within a few minutes of four steam railway stations at Newton Centre, West Newton, Newtonville and Newton Highlands, respectively. Bullough's Pond Park is one of Newton's newest park enterprises and is to be completed this season. It is in one of the most picturesque localities of the " Garden City," and the city has so dredged and improved the pond and watercourse that the locality will necessarily be one of the most healthful. Substantially all the lands about Bullough's Pond Park are owned by the New-ton Land and Improvment Company, and many fine residences have been erected here, while others are contemplated. The Newton Land and Improvement Company still retains the most beautiful sites on the Park, on Commonwealth Avenue and Walnut Street, as well as on numerous other streets overlooking the park and Commonwealth Avenue. (See Page 74.) This is one of the few large tracts in the vicinity of Boston (about 125 acres) which is so restricted that none but a desirable class of structures will be erected on it. It is provided not only with a network of steam and electric roads, but with all modern im-provements, and is a most desirable locality. The Commonwealth Avenue Street Railway runs from this point westerly over West Newton Heights, along the boulevard. At Chestnut Street there are groves on both sides and as the car goes on through sylvan scenery, it passes a little stile on the left marked " Bræburn Golf Club," where lovers of the ancient game may often be seen playing. Soon Washington Street,

AUBURNDALE, is reached, where connection may be made with cars for Newton Lower Falls, Wellesley and points beyond, on the left, while on the right the cars run to West Newton and Waltham or Newtonville. At the left, just beyond Washington Street, is the famous Woodland Park Hotel, with its spacious and well-kept grounds and golf links. Here coaching parties often run out from the City for din-ners at the hotel. Continuing on the Commonwealth Avenue line the car soon comes to the terminus at

NORUMBEGA PARK, which is controlled by the enterprising Commonwealth Avenue Street Railway Company. This place combines all the attractive features of a public park, while its freedom from objectionable characters and its admirable management make it more exclusive than any public ground. Opened two years ago, it has from the first attracted a superior class of patrons, owing to its excellent management, while it possesses two distinct advan-

ENTRANCE TO NORUMBEGA PARK.

tages over other parks in its nearness to the million people of Greater Boston and its picturesque location on the beautiful Charles River. Planned and laid out by an experienced landscape gardener, the natural advantages of the place have been utilized in full. The Commonwealth Avenue Street Railway cars discharge passengers within the grounds, entering a picturesque two-story pavilion, the lower floor of which is utilized for offices, car storage, etc., while the upper floor is on a level with the park. With one part open on the park side for use in pleasant weather, the upper floor of the pavilion has a dining hall with accommodations for 350 people. The luncheons and dinners served here are well known to Boston tourists and all who visit the park may be assured that the comfort of the inner man will be well looked after.

Norumbega Park itself comprises about twelve acres of ground, most of which is at an elevation of

OPEN AIR THEATRE.

thirty or thirty-five feet above the river, on which the park has a frontage of 2,200 feet. In addition to the pavilion, there is a boathouse near the entrance, the finest structure of the kind to be found on the Charles River. Here is a large fleet of rowboats, canoes and launches, and in addition to the stabling for boats there are ample lockers and toilet rooms. Another building is a bicycle house, accommodating hundreds of wheels, with a repair shop attached. Scattered about the grounds are many little pavilions where ladies may sit, free from annoyance, while their children play in clean sand piles provided for their special entertainment. On the highest ground in the park is a band stand, where summer evening concerts are given by some of the best bands in the state. Another feature is the open-air theatre, with 1,500 free seats, where a high-class stage entertainment is provided every afternoon and evening except Sunday, in summer. Down in the woods, along the river bank, is a deer park and the largest zoological collection in New England, with animals not to be found in any other open park in this country. In one part of the park is an electric fountain, where, every evening, myriad jets of water spring into the air to fall in a shower of prismatic gems. The usual park attractions, rustic seats, swings, merry-go-rounds, donkey carriages, etc., are provided.

With all that has been done, however, the natural beauties of the park have been admirably conserved. Here it is that the Charles River broadens out and runs into delightful nooks and eddies where the canoeist loves to linger. Groves of stately trees arise on either side, and the glimpses of the river through the woods in the park attract many amateur photographers. An easy row up the river brings one to Riverside, where are the boat houses of the Newton Boat Club, the country home of the Boston Athletic Association and the grounds of the Associated Athletic Clubs. Down stream there are many delightful views at every turn, with the park as the crowning feature, on the right. Across the river, in Weston is the historic Norumbega Tower, from which the park takes its name. This grey stone tower was erected to commemorate the discovery, on this spot, of relics of the followers of Lief Ericksen and Thorwald, the Norseman, who founded the colony of Norumbega here about the year 1000. For all these points of interest Norumbega is the natural starting point of tourists. The experience of the past year has shown the management the value of making this street railway park a place where ladies and children may go with perfect safety, and the public has learned that no street railway trip around Boston is more delightful than that to Norumbega.

NORUMBEGA TOWER

Through the Newtons.

Echo Bridge.

ONE of the most popular trolley trips from Boston is that to Hemlock Gorge Reservation and Echo Bridge at Newton Upper Falls, reached by the Newton & Boston Street Railway. One may go out from Boston to Newtonville, or by a longer trip through Cambridge and Watertown, past Harvard College and Mount Auburn Cemetery. The Boston cars stop at Watertown Square, from which a branch line runs to the United States Arsenal, passing the great Brighton Union Stock Market.

Other branches run to Waltham and Newton. Going to Echo Bridge, the car crosses Charles River near what is said to have been the home of the Norsemen who discovered America before Columbus. On the right of the bridge is a tablet which bears the inscription :

"OUTLOOK UPON THE STONE DAM

AND STONE-WALLED

DOCKS AND WHARVES OF NORUMBEGA,

THE SEAPORT OF

THE NORTHMEN IN VINLAND."

On the left the tablet reads:

"THE OLD BRIDGE BY THE MILL

CROSSED CHARLES RIVER NEAR THIS SPOT

AS EARLY AS 1861."

The tablets were put up by Professor Eben N. Horsford, the distinguished antiquarian scholar. Passing, on Watertown street, an old house where General Washington once stopped, the car runs through Nonantum, where a change may be made for Waltham (via Bemis), or Newton. Running past Silver Lake.

NEWTONVILLE is entered. The car passes the Adams School, the Central Congregational Church and goes over the Boston & Albany railroad tracks. Beyond, it goes past the Methodist Episcopal Church on the left, the Newton Club on the right, then the Claflin School on the left and the Newton High School beyond, on the other side. Just beyond this is "The Elms," the home of Ex-Governor Claflin. A few minutes later one comes to the Newton Boulevard Waiting Station, and then passing Newton Cemetery and many pretty houses, reaches

NEWTON HIGHLANDS. Here the car turns to the right and runs past the Congregational Church and the Grammar School, and after a couple of turns runs through the woods and across country to

NEWTON UPPER FALLS. At this place the car makes a wide sweep around three streets, the view from High street being extensive and beautiful. Leaving the car and going down the Charles River banks, one comes to Echo Bridge, the aqueduct which carries the Boston water supply across the Charles River. Near the water, at the end of the bridge, there is a famous repeating echo. The State park reserva-

ECHO BRIDGE.

tion is across the river. The street car line continues from Newton Upper Falls past the Newton Silk Mills, crosses the river above the falls, and runs between the Charles River on the left and the high aqueduct on the right, to Highlandville. From here it runs through fields and woods, climbing a hill from which is a fine view, before coming to Needham, the terminus of the line, connecting with lines for Boston, Wellesley and beyond.

Through the Newtons.

Prospect Hill.

A NOTHER ride on the electric cars through another part of the Newtons, to Prospect Hill, in Waltham, returning through Cambridge, takes the pleasure-seeker through a great diversity of scenery to the highest elevation near Boston that can be reached by electric car. The car marked Commonwealth avenue, Brighton and Newton may be taken in the subway or at Copley square in Boston, the route running through the Back Bay residence district Commonwealth avenue, Allston and Brighton to Nonantum Square, Newton by the route described under Boston trips. At

NEWTON a change is made to the cars of the Newton Street Railway Company, for Newtonville, West Newton and Waltham. A line also runs from here to Watertown. The car taken on this trip goes past Mount Ida and enters

NEWTONVILLE, where one line runs to Newton Upper Falls, while the car for Prospect Hill passes the new Masonic Temple and goes on through a pretty part of the "Garden City," to

WEST NEWTON. Here a line runs to Auburndale, so that one may go by this way to Norumbega Park. The City Hall, an unpretentious wooden building on the right, is passed on the way to

WALTHAM. As the line is neared the Charles River is seen on the left, and the car passes the factory of the Waltham Manufacturing Company. Crossing the River just beyond, the Boston Manufacturing Company's Mills, the first in America to make cotton cloth direct from the raw material, are seen. Here the late General Banks was once employed as a bobbin boy. At this point the Fitchburg Railroad tracks are crossed and one comes to Waltham Common, and continues up Main street passing the Banks' homestead and stops at the foot of Prospect Hill, which the city of Waltham has set apart as a public ground under the name of

GENERAL BANKS' HOMESTEAD.

PROSPECT HILL PARK. A walk for fifteen minutes, at an easy pace, brings one to the summit of Prospect Hill, the view from which is the finest in eastern Massachusetts. Below is a fine view of the winding Charles River and its valley, with the world-famous American Waltham Watch Company's factory along its banks. Beginning in the west with noble Mount Wachusett in Princeton, as the eye turns to the north it views the round knob of Watatick in Ashburnham, then comes to Mount Monadnock, in Jaffrey, N. H., then come the Kidder or Peterboro Mountains, beautiful with their double summits; beyond and to the north will be seen the Lyndeborough Mountains. with the Crotchet Mountain peak in Francestown, N. H., above the

AMERICAN WALTHAM WATCH CO'S. FACTORY.

top of the range, and then is further to the right the stony pile in New Boston, N. H., known as Joe English Hill. Still to the right are the twin peaks of Unconoonuc Mountains in Golfstown, N. H., and with an ordinary opera glass, one may see westerly flank of the West Unconoonuc, Mount Kearsarge. in Central New Hampshire.

Leaving the hill and going back to Waltham Common a change is made, the car running first through the business district of Waltham, and thence, into the best residence section, along a well shaded street. Grove Hill Cemetery is passed on the right, and then the car runs into

WATERTOWN, going through a farming district until the village is entered suddenly. From here the route back to Boston is by way of Mount Auburn street, through Cambridge, passing Mount Auburn Cemetery, Elmwood, Longfellow's Park and Harvard College, as described under one of the Boston trips by trolley.

A South Country Trip.

SOUTH of Boston lies a country rich alike in natural scenery and historic associations. West Roxbury and Roslindale, two beautiful suburbs of Boston, and the pretty towns of Dedham, Norwood and Walpole are reached by taking the Boston Elevated cars marked Forest Hills, at which point direct connection is made with cars of the West Roxbury & Roslindale Street Railway Company for a delightful trip through town and country. Cars marked "Forest Hills,Dedham, Norwood and EastWalpole"run through without change.

HIGH SERVICE OBSERVATORY, STONY BROOK
RESERVATION,

At Forest Hills, on the left, are the entrances to Franklin Park and Forest Hills Cemetery, and on the right is the fine viaduct of the New York, New Haven, & Hartford Railway. The car goes up easy grades, past the High Service Pumping Station of the Boston Water Works, and the high service tower and observatory, which has an elevation of 375 feet above the level of the sea, and from which one of the finest views in the vicinity of Boston is to be had. One can look seaward for twenty-five miles; westerly to Mount Monadnock, some sixty-three miles; southerly as far as Franklin, seventeen miles, and northerly as far as Holt's Hill, Andover, about twenty-five

VIEW FROM STONY BROOK RESERVATION, SHOWING TURTLE POND, NEPONSET VALLEY, AND BLUE HILL.

miles. This tower is in the Stony Brook Reservation of the Metropolitan Park System, through which the car runs for nearly a mile, bringing within easy access of Boston this extensive wooded park, excellent views being afforded of the Blue Hills in Milton, Turtle Pond and the Neponset Valley. On every side are charming sylvan glimpses. Passing the pretty Mother Brook, on the edge of the Reservation, the car enters

DEDHAM,
crossing the
car tracks at
Crove street
and reaching
the southern
terminus of the
line at Memo-
rial Sqaure,
where the Nor-
folk Central
Street Railway
begins. It is

HISTORICAL BUILDING, DEDHAM.

well to stop over a car in Dedham, for this is one of
the finest of the old New England colonial towns.
A convenient and well-kept waiting-room at this point
is at the disposal of patrons of both roads. Opposite
the waiting-room is the Memorial Hall, and just
above this is the Historical Building, in which are
placed many interesting relics of early Dedham. A
visit well repays one, for an atmosphere of the past per-
vades the town
which is over
210 years old
and has much
of historic in-
terest to show
visitors. Near
by is seen the
Public Library
and almost op-
posite this is
the new Nor-
folk County

PUBLIC LIBRARY, DEDHAM.

Court House, a building of truly magnificent proportions.

The boathouse of the Dedham Boat Club is within

OLD POWDER HOUSE ON POWDER HOUSE ROCK, DEDHAM.

easy walking distance, and from here a charming view of the upper Charles River may be had. Within sight of the boathouse is Powder House Rock, on which

BOAT HOUSE, DEDHAM BOAT CLUB.

still stands the old Powder House, erected in the seventeenth century, when every town was required to keep on hand a stock of powder for the use of its citizens in repulsing invading hostile forces.

From the waiting station, in another direction, a walk of half a mile brings one to the historic Fairbanks House, built in the year 1636 by Jonathan Fairbanks, and maintained in its original form by the

OLD FAIRBANKS HOUSE.

Daughters of the Revolution. There are many other historical points to be reached by short walks or drives in Dedham, and the new part of the town is picturesque and inviting.

Resuming the journey, on the Norfolk Central trolley car, the way leads to Islington, past Westwood Park. Entertainments of many kinds are furnished here in summer, and posters on the street cars will inform passengers of the different attractions. The links of the Norfolk Golf Club are easily reached from here. Continuing on, one comes to Norwood, a pretty rural village in which the old tavern, the handsome Unitarian Church, and the great Norwood Press

OLD TAVERN, NORWOOD.

are among the sights to attract the attention of visitors. From Norwood the cars continue on to

EAST WALPOLE, at the Bird Memorial, erected in honor of the late T. W. Bird, known widely

WESTWOOD PARK, BROOK SCENE.

as the "Sage of Walpole." Here are located the paper
mills of Bird & Company, Hollingsworth & Vose, and
other manufacturers. Many enjoyable walks may be
taken, if one desires to remain over a car or two.
From here the cars run on to the terminus of the line
at Walpole, a pretty New England manufacturing village, and a railroad junction point.

The return journey to Dedham is made over the
same route, but from there to Boston other scenery
may' be enjoyed by going over the West Roxbury
division of the West Roxbury & Roslindale Street
Railway, taking a transfer at Grove street to East
Dedham. Many pretty views of river scenery may be
had. Here also one may see the stone which marks
the site of the first mill and dam on the Charles River,
built in 1640. Taking the car on its return journey to
Forest Hills, one goes by the West Roxbury division.

The time occupied by the trip from Forest Hills
and return, as here outlined, is about three hours,
and the fares are only thirty cents. The ride is
through city, town and country, with ever-varying
scenery delighting the passenger. Of course a whole
day may profitably be taken for the trip, stopping
over to visit other points of interest in the country
traversed.

Another South County trip by the Needham &
Boston Street Railway Co. may be taken after the
early summer. It takes the traveler from Forest
Hills over the lines of the West Roxbury & Roslindale Street Railway as far as Spring Street, then
up the Charles River to Needham, where connections can be made with the cars for Newton, Wellesley, Natick, Framingham, Marlboro and Worcester.
The cars turn off from the Dedham line at Spring

street, passing near the Caledonian Club, the boat houses and the free public baths. It is only a short ride to Dedham Island Hill, from which a fine view is had of Needham, Newton, Brookline and the valley of the Charles below. Going down the hill to the valley, the Charles is followed for nearly a mile, the car running along broad meadows, across which are beautiful views. The car passes in sight of "Karlstein," the handsome country place of Samuel D. Warren, with its golf links and famous polo grounds. Then the way leads through the new and attractive village of Oakhurst (see page 60), where the car runs on a wide boulevard and thence through Needham, to the terminus of the line at Needham Centre.

From Norwood a line has just been completed southward to Walpole, Foxboro, Mansfield, Attleboro or Providence; a change is made at Norwood Centre to the car of the Norfolk Southern Street Railway Company. The route runs past the Morrill Memorial Library, a handsome granite building on the right, and then follows along the new state highway now in course of construction. Running on toward East Walpole, there is another view of the Blue Hills in Milton, surmounted by its weather observatory, and the car enters

WALPOLE. This town is a pretty one, with a Common in the centre, around which are grouped magnificent oak and elm trees. Passing the Town Hall on the left, the trees on either side of the street form an archway of verdure through which the car runs for some distance. Another turn is made to the left, and the car runs on Washington street into the village of South Walpole. Before entering the village

the Water Tower which supplies water to this district is seen looming up in the distance. From here
a branch line runs northerly to connect with the line
of the Norfolk Central Street Railway at East Walpole, the journey to which has already been described.
In the centre of the town are the remains of the two
old taverns which were once famous hostelries, rival
half-way houses on the stage road from Boston to
Providence before the days of the steam railroad and
the trolley car. The old Polly Tavern was on the
right, and Fuller's Tavern on the left. Passing by
these relics of the olden time, the car leaves the old
post road for the last time, and runs into the town of

FOXBORO. This is a picturesque town with
a pleasant park and a handsome granite Memorial
Building erected in honor of its dead soldiers, and used
as a public library. The town is engaged in the manufacture of straw hats and bonnets. The car passes first
through North Foxboro and then through West Foxboro, where a branch line running off to the right
takes one to Lake Pearl. This is much patronized
by picnic parties and pleasure-seekers in summer.
Running through Foxboro another double row of
fine old trees arches the roadway. Emerging into
the open country, there is a run for some distance between farm fields before one enters

MANSFIELD, the terminus of the line. Mansfield is the centre of a farming region, and has several
small factories, with diversified industries. Here connections are made with electric cars for Brockton,
Taunton, Norton, Attleboro and Providence.

A South Country Trip II.

— —

IN addition to the line previously mentioned, the cars of the Norfolk Suburban Street Railway run from the Forest Hills terminus of the Boston Elevated Railway Company, southward to Dedham. This line runs along Washington street, with the Arnold Arboretum on the right and Forest Hills Cemetery on the left. After leaving these. the ride is through a pleasant valley, with Mount Hope Cemetery off to the left, and soon Hyde Park township is entered at Clarendon Hills. Then a more distinctively rural country is seen, and keeping in sight the wooded range of hills on the right all the way, the car runs into

HYDE PARK CENTRE. Here connections are made with the cars for Readville and Mattapan. The Readville branch runs due south, entering the town which was the camp of the Massachusetts volunteers in the Civil War, and now famous for its trotting track, where the New England Breeders' Association holds its meetings. From Readville there is a splendid near view of the Blue Hills. The Dedham car from Hyde Park turns to the right, crossing the tracks of the New York, New Haven & Hartford Railroad, and entering the residence district known

99

as Sunnyside. On the left are the fine Harlow and
Brainerd residences, and on the right the Cotter place.
In the distance is seen the home of Robert Blaikie,
the woolen manufacturer.

Passing the woolen mill, the power house and
other plants in the manufacturing district, the car
leaves on the right the road to Fairview Cemetery,
beyond which is the Stony Brook Reservation of the
Metropolitan Park System. Crossing Cotton Mill
Pond, a widening of Mother Brook, there is a fine
view of the Blue Hills, which are still blue in spite of
their nearness, and on the top of Great Blue Hill may
be seen the weather observatory and kite-flying station. Mother Brook is interesting from the fact that
it rises in one stream, the Charles River, and flows
into another, the Neponset, really making Boston an
island.

Turning to the right into Readville street, the car
runs by the Cochrane Print Works, situated in the
valley below the highway. Passing other mills, it
then comes into East Dedham Square, just beyond
which is the Avery School building. Then the traveler goes by the famous Chelsea Pottery Works and
a large wool-scouring mill, and then passing the large
stone Catholic Church, runs by picturesque old houses
and under the tracks of the New York, New Haven &
Hartford Railroad, to come to the terminus in Memorial Square, Dedham. Here connections may be
made for West Roxbury, Norwood, Walpole, Medfield and East Walpole.

MATTAPAN and Milton Lower Mills are
reached from Hyde Park by making a transfer to the
line which runs to the left on River street. Leaving

the business centre of Hyde Park, passing the stone
edifice of Christ Church on the right, and going by
the fountain and band stand in Hyde Park Square, the
car runs on East River street between comfortable
residences with well-kept grounds. The Butler
School is passed on the left, and on the right is a new
residence district, on what was once the handsome
Summer estate.

Just beyond, on the same side, are the Tileston
and Hollingsworth "Mattapan Mills," where fine
writing paper is made. Passing the entrance to the
new settlement of Rugby on the left before crossing
the tracks of the Midland Division of the New Haven
Railroad, the plant of the Boston Gossamer Rubber
Works is seen on the right, with its well-kept grounds
and flower beds. Going by the Colonial residence of
John P. Ray on the left, the new residence district of
Holmfield is seen on the opposite side. Just beyond
is the dividing line between Boston and Hyde Park,
marked by an old house, part of which is in the city,
and part in the town. A short run brings the traveler
to

MATTAPAN, at the junction of Blue Hill avenue, Norfolk street and Brushy Hill Road, known as
Mattapan Square. Here is the railroad station on the
right, and crossing the Neponset River bridge just
beyond, on the right, a short walk brings one into an
avenue of noble old elms, with fine views on every
side. A walk on Blue Hill avenue for half a mile
brings one to Walk Hill street, where cars of the Boston Elevated Railway may be taken for the city passing the Home for Aged Hebrews and Franklin Park
before reaching Grove Hall transfer station.

The street railway line from Mattapan continues
down East River street, going past a starch factory
and an old cotton mill on the right before entering
Milton Lower Mills. The car also passes the great
Baker Chocolate Mills before reaching the terminus
of the line, where connection may be made with the·
Boston Elevated Railway cars for the city, via Field's
Corner.

Through Blue Hill Reservation.

THE greatest of the state park reservations is the
Blue Hill Reservation in Milton.   Heretofore
it has been reached only with difficulty, but the
line of the Boston, Milton & Brockton Street Railway,
now under construction and to be opened about July
1, brings this magnificent stretch of country within
easy reach of the city. The Reservation includes forests, fields, meadows, hills, valleys, swamps, rivers ; in
fact an almost endless diversity of natural scenery
within its borders, which include more than five thousand acres. To reach it, one should take a Milton
Lower Mills car of the Boston Elevated Railway, going over the route described under the Boston trolley
trips.

At the Neponset River a change is made to the
Boston. Milton & Brockton car, which runs through
the town of Milton in a wide reserved way, with a
good macadam road on either side of the tracks. Milton is famed for its well kept residences of wealthy
gentlemen, and the various styles of architecture, with
wide lawns running down from the residences to the
roadway, make a pleasing picture. The car touches

the Blue Hill Reservation on the left, after leaving
the town, and soon plunges into it, running for nearly
two miles through the beautiful sylvan scenery of the
great state park. The ride is between Chickatawbut
Hill on the left and Hancock Hill on the right. Beyond Hancock Hill is Great Blue Hill, with its weather observatory and the famous government kite-flying
station. It can be reached from the car line by a walk
along the woodland paths. Leaving the Reservation
the car runs into Randolph, Great Pond being off to
the left before the car enters the village, where connections may be made with the Brockton Street Railway cars for Highland Park, Brockton and points
beyond.

Transfers on the Milton cars at the corner of
Readsville road and Randolph avenue in Milton al-
low passengers to take a branch line running off to
East Milton. At this point connections may be made
with the Quincy & Boston Street Railway for Quincy
and Nantasket Beach, and points described under
"Along the South Shore," or "Into the Old Colony."

A South Country Trip III.

IT will well repay anyone who makes the trolley trip to Dedham to continue the journey over the line of the Norfolk Western Street Railway to Westwood and Medfield, by changing at Memorial Square, from either the cars of the West Roxbury & Roslindale, the Norfolk Suburban or the Norfolk Central Street Railway lines. The cars of the Norfolk Western run through High street, in Dedham, passing the pillar erected by the Sons of Liberty and the splendid new granite Norfolk County Court House. After running through the settled part of the town, the car leaves the pretty street to enter pleasant groves, through which it runs for some distance. Emerging into the open, on the left, near White's Pond, is the old Town Pound, and running on, the traveler finds himself upon a hill in the centre of the new town of

WESTWOOD, recently set off from Dedham as a separate town. From the elevation, the Blue Hills of Milton are clearly seen, off to the left, while below is spread out an entrancing panorama of scenery in the valley and the meadows. Westwood is an exceedingly pretty town, with an abundant growth of shade trees. On Main street, just before entering the town, the car passes the old Colburn House built before 1700. Off to the left may be seen Fox Hill, upon which are the summer homes of many of the well-known families of Boston. Continuing on, still in the town of Westwood, one passes, to the left, the Reservoir and Pumping Station belonging to the town of Norwood. After leaving the town of Westwood, on the right, the car passes a hemlock tree known as the "witch tree" from the fact that Moll Pitcher once slept under its boughs. Here is one of the most picturesque waiting stations

COLBURN HOUSE, WESTWOOD

to be found on all the network of street railways in Eastern Massachusetts. It was built of rough field stone collected in the neighborhood, and has an old-fashioned fireplace of the same material inside. Here the passenger may obtain refreshments before continuing his journey. The ride from Westood is through a typical New England farming country with the old-fashioned farmhouses and ample barns as a feature of the landscape. It is only a short run from the waiting station to King Philip's Park, so called, because it is situated on historic ground in the town

of Medfield, once a part of the domain of the famous
Indian sachem. The park consists of some two
hundred acres, recently acquired by the street railway company, and beautifully adapted to the wants
of the pleasure-seeker. The tract is well shaded,
and a brook winds its way through the park over the
rocks and ledges. The company put a large force
of men at work in the park, clearing up the under-
brush, this spring, and it is expected that by the first

HIGH STREET, WESTWOOD.

of July the place will be open to the public. An
artificial pond of more than sixty acres in extent will
be made in the park, and on the edge of this a chute
will be erected. Throughout the park the best of
the natural features will be preserved, but there
will be special attractions, such as a dancing pavilion, swings, rustic seats and refreshment stands,
especial attention being paid to clambakes in the
summer time. After leaving the park there is
another run through more rural country, and then
the traveler comes to

MEDFIELD, with its fine residences, each with its generous lawn in front, and shaded by large trees. As the car enters the town one may see on the right, a weather-beaten house said to be the only one left in Medfield after the massacre and burning of the town in King Philip's War. On this trip, instead of using the common way, the company has acquired a right of way beside the main road, nearly the entire distance, so that it will be possible to run these cars much faster than those on most street railway lines. At present, the terminus is near the centre of the town, but by the first of August it is expected to have the line extended as far as Medway, where connections may be made with Milford, Hopedale, etc., allowing the passenger to return to Boston by an entirely different route. It will be difficult to find a more pleasant street railway trip in any part of New England, and the section of the country traversed is such that the traveler will obtain not only a succession of delightful views, but will gain an excellent idea of the industries, farms and pretty inland towns for which Massachusetts is noted.

R. H. DERRAH

MAKES A
SPECIALTY OF

TROLLEY EXCURSIONS

On the Famous North Shore.

NO part of Massachusetts is more famous for its scenic beauty than that lying along the coast of Massachusetts Bay, from Boston to the tip end of Cape Ann, the summer home of many wealthy residents of Eastern cities and the Riviera of New England,—the North Shore. It embraces within its limits many towns and cities famous for the deeds of their citizens in the early days of our country. But while the towns and cities have grown, a new population has sprung up in this section, a population of dwellers in the cities who come here to find beautiful homes amid the finest of natural surroundings. A series of summer resorts has been developed, and the electric railway has bound all these together, so that one may journey by trolley all the way from Boston to the end of the Cape, with many pleasant side trips from Lynn, Salem and Beverly.

Starting from Boston in the Subway at Scollay, Adams or Haymarket Squares or at the North Union Station on a Lynn & Boston car, the ride is first through Charlestown, then across the Mystic and through Chelsea and Revere on the route described under Boston trips in going to Revere Beach Reservation. Instead, however, of going to the beach, the Lynn & Boston car keeps on Broadway and passing two streets where lines diverge, one to the left to Malden and another on the right to the upper end of Revere Beach, it goes over the salt marshes of Saugus town. Here the tide water fills the inlets of the marsh, across which on the right, may be seen the shining waters of the Bay. Going over the Saugus River drawbridge the car enters

LYNN. Across the marshes may be seen the

BATHING AT REVERE.

city spires and tall chimneys, and on the right is the great plant of the General Electric Works, Lynn now being one of the greatest electrical centres of the country. Entering Lynn Common and passing along South Common Street one may see, on the right, the oldest church in Lynn, and the new Armory, before passing the splendid City Hall and going through the district burned over in the great fire of November, 1889, into Central Square, which is the terminus for lines of the Lynn & Boston Railroad Company which run in all directions,

Wherever one may go, shoe manufacturing establishments, for which Lynn is world-famous, may be seen. The branch lines running out of Lynn bring in communication with the city the neighboring places of historic interest, the city and state parks, the meadows and marshes of the lowlands, the groves and views of the hills and the rocky shores and sandy beaches of the coast. One of the pleasantest of these side trips is that to

LYNN WOODS.

LYNN WOODS, connecting with lines for Wakefield, Reading and Lowell. Taking a Lynnhurst car, going first through the business and manufacturing districts, and then through the residence part of the city, the traveler passes the Reservoir and Pumping Station and Breed's Pond, on the left, before arriving at the main entrance to Lynn Woods. This is a part of the Metropolitan Park System, and the largest pleasure ground, in proportion to population, adjoining any city in the country. The park has many

attractions for the
trolley tourist, and
one may well spend
a day here.

LYNN WOODS.

Within the limits
of Lynn Woods are
four beautiful sheets
of water Glen-Lewis,
Walden, Breed's and
Birch Ponds, and
miles of cool walks,
which make this a favorite picnic ground. Among the
popular attractions of the park is famous Dungeon
Rock, which tradition says was an ancient haunt of
pirates. Here is a cave painfully wrought in the hard
porphyry by Hiram Marble, a hermit who sought
for gold, claiming to work under spiritual guidance.

From Lynn Woods cars may be taken on to Wakefield, through North Saugus. To those wishing to return to Lynn another way, a walk across to Glen-Lewis
Pond will bring one to the Lynn cars running back by
Wyoma Lake, Wyoma Village and Chestnut Street.

NAHANT BEACH, one of the finest summer
resorts on the North
Shore, famed for its
fish dinners, boating
and seashore attrac-
tions, is within a half-
mile run of the city,
reached by another
electric line from the
Central Square or
at the Railroad Sta-
tion.

CLIFTONDALE and Malden are reached by a branch from the Square, the car running through a pretty, open farming country in the town of Saugus, and then going through the villages of East Saugus and Cliftondale, and passing Franklin Park, with its trotting track, before entering the suburbs of Malden.

BOARDMAN HOUSE, SAUGUS. BUILT IN 1700.

EAST SAUGUS, Saugus Centre and Melrose are on a branch running from Lynn through a country of market gardens, orchards and farms, offering a most enjoyable trip for lovers of country scenes.

PEABODY and **DANVERS** contain much that is of interest to the trolley excursionist, and both these towns are reached by branches from Lynn as well as from Salem. The lover of antiquities especially will find much to delight him, as both are quaint old towns. The route from Central Square, Lynn, leads through a region of delightful landscapes after leaving the business part of the city, passing Spring, Brown's and Bartholomew Ponds, with their semi-public picnic grounds. At Bartholomew Pond, a short walk from the electric line, is Ship Rock, the largest boulder in this part of the coontry, and much visited by geologists and others. Going through South Peabody and passing Flax Pond, the car enters Peabody, once a part of Danvers, and named in honor of George Peabody, the great London banker and philanthropist, who was born here. The Peabody Institute, on

PEABODY INSTITUTE, PEABODY.

Main street, contains many interesting relics of Peabody's distinguished son, including the portrait of herself given to him by Queen Victoria. In the Square is the monument to the minute-men of Peabody and Danvers, and near by the site of the famous Bell Tavern and the ancient cemetery.

From Peabody the line continues to Danvers, which was settled in 1628. Here the witchcraft delusion raged in 1692, and the Rebecca Nourse house, the home of one of its victims, is still standing. Here, also, is the home of General Israel Putnam, "Old Put" of Revolutionary fame, on Centre street, and "Oak Knoll," Whittier's home, on Summer street. From here a line of cars run to Asylum station, at the foot of a high hill on which the State Insane Asylum is located. Another line branches to the left, to Danvers Centre, and a third runs to Putnamville, from which the traveler may go to Danvers and Danversport, or by way of Peabody to Salem.

REBECCA NOURSE HOUSE, DANVERS.   BUILT IN 1630.

MARBLEHEAD and SWAMPSCOTT are on one of the lines running from Lynn to Salem, and this route is recommended to one who loves the seashore. Old Marblehead is one of the quaintest, most delightful towns in the world, and the scenery on this route has an ever-changing charm. From Central Square, Lynn, the ride is along the magnificent boulevards known as Broad and Lewis streets, and leaving the residence district of Lynn and crossing the line into Swampscott, the electric car skirts the coast, with a view of the open sea on the right, surf breaking on the rocks below and here and there a shining sail on the distant blue. From the historic hay-scales in Swampscott to the end of the route, the ride is one of unfailing interest.

Near at hand, on the left, are handsome summer cottages, while on the right the car runs along the open sea, past King's Beach, with fine surf bathing, now a state reservation. Egg Rock, with its light-

FOUNTAIN INN AND AGNES SURRAGE WELL, MARBLEHEAD.

house, is seen across the water, and running past Beach Bluff and the little village of Clifton Heights, the car enters the crooked streets of old Marblehead, where connections may be made with barges and the steam ferry for Marblehead Neck, a noted pleasure resort. The car runs on to the end of the town to Fort Sewall, where there are pleasure grounds and a magnificent ocean view.

Marblehead of today is largely a town of delightful

summer homes, but contains much that is old and picturesque. The early settlers laid out their streets in
zigzag fashion over the rocks, and these streets remain, with here and there some of the old-time houses.
Marblehead formed a part of Salem until 1648, being
foremost among the coast towns of Massachusetts in
the fishing industry. Off the shore of Old Fort Sewall some of the most important naval engagements of

TUCKER LANDING, MARBLEHEAD.

the Revolution took place. The old Town House
was built in 1727, and Abbott Hall, one of the land-
marks of the town, contains many interesting historical objects, including the famous painting: "The
Spirit of '76." At the lower end of the town on Orne
street are the Fountain Inn, scene of the novel, "Agnes
Surriage," and Old Burying Hill. Near the road to
Marblehead Neck is Cow Fort, erected in Revolutionary days, and at the fork of the road near the Lynn &
Boston car houses was once an old Indian fort. On
the same street with Abbott Hall is the historic

church of St. Michael, built in 1714, and a short distance below is the residence of Elbridge Gerry. From Marblehead the trip may be made direct to Salem.

From Lynn the direct ride to Salem is made from Central Square by taking a car marked "Lynn and Salem." The car runs along Essex and Union streets, and through Upper Swampscott, crossing the railroad track and passing the Swampscott Cemetery, and on the right the White Lead Wokrs. It is a pleasant ride

MARBLEHEAD NECK.

all the way, and after passing the mills and crossing the railroad tracks again, the car runs past fine residences along Lafayette street, South Salem, and reaches the terminus near the Salem City Hall. Like Lynn, Salem is a street railway centre, and some of the branch lines may be considered before resuming the journey on the main line.

SALEM WILLOWS is a popular seashore resort, kept as a public park, with various attractions

SALEM WILLOWS.

and band concerts on Wednesdays and Sundays. Its crowning feature is an avenue of noble elms from which it takes its name. On the way to the Willows the car passes the East India Marine Hall and the Essex Institute, and their collections which speak of Salem's former maritime greatness, and comes to Salem Neck, over which it passes with views of the water on both sides. Approaching the Willows, the City Almshouse and Farm are passed on the right. Beyond the hospital on the left are the ruins of old Fort Lee, built in 1699. The frigate "Essex," of the War of 1812, was built at Salem Willows. Opposite the cove are the ruins of old Fort Pickering and Winter Island, most of which is used by the Plummer Farm School, the government retaining the rest.

As has been mentioned, other branches from Salem run to Marblehead, Peabody and Danvers. People going to Salem

GENERAL PUTNAM'S HOUSE, DANVERS.

from Lynn by the inland route, should return via Marblehead and Swampscott. The visitor in Salem will see much that is of interest by taking short walks, for this was the mother city of the Massachusetts Colony, founded In 1623, before Boston, was a town; here was the home of Hawthorne, Bancroft and other men of letters; here the witchcraft delusion reached its height, and from here the ships of Salem once sailed to the remotest parts of the globe.

HOUSE OF SEVEN GABLES, SALEM.

Of the historic houses, that of Roger Williams is on the corner of North and Essex streets; the Shuttuck house, of witchcraft fame, is at 317 Essex street; the Pickering Mansion, built in 1649, is at 18 Broad street, and the house visited by Lafayette in 1784, and by Washington in 1789, is at 138 Federal street. Hawthorne's birthplace was at 21 Union street, and the House of the Seven Gables is at 64 Turner street. Gallows Hill, where those convicted of witchcraft were executed, is at the head of Hanson street.

Leaving historic Salem to resume the journey on the main line to Gloucester and beyond, a change is made to a Beverly car, which runs down Essex street. In Derby Square, on the right, is the Salem Town Hall and Market, built in 1816, and just beyond is the East India Marine Hall and Peabody Academy of Science, open to visitors free on week-days and containing, besides a large collection of scientific specimens, many interesting models of naval architecture.

A little further on, on the left, are three buildings, the Cadet Hall, the Salem Athenæum, containing a large library, and the Essex Institute, with its valuable historical collections. Back of the Athenæum is the first church erected in New England, of which Roger Williams was pastor. From here a short and pleasant ride brings one to Essex Bridge, with beautiful views east and west. Here Washington left his carriage to enjoy the views, when on his way from Salem to Beverly to visit Hon. George Cabot. Crossing the Bridge the car enters

BEVERLY. This is largely a summer town, with many fine avenues leading down to the ocean on the right, or stretching back into inviting groves on the left. It is a more quiet and less pretentious summer resort than some others on the North Shore, but it is none the less beautiful. A branch line runs from here to

BEVERLY COVE, the oldest of the summer resorts along this part of the country, famed alike for the beauty of its scenery and its fine residences. The electric line winds through Hale street, along the shore and then through shady groves. From a point near the terminus of the line an unsurpassed sea view is obtained.

WENHAM and **ASBURY GROVE** are also reached by a branch line from Beverly, the trip being an especially pleasant one. There are great estates with handsome country houses, and little farmhouses with shoe shops attached, reminders of the days when shoes were finished in the homes of the

WENHAM LAKE.

workers, before the time of the great factories. Wenham Lake, a beautiful sheet of water, is passed, and after going near the golf links of the Myopia Hunt Club the car comes to Wenham and Hamilton railway station, a short distance from this fashionable North Shore country club. It is a short ride to Asbury Grove, noted as a summer resort and as a place of the annual Methodist camp meetings.

The car from Salem to Beverly stops on Cabot

street in Beverly, running up alongside the car of the
Gloucester, Essex & Beverly Street Railway Company. Past the Briscoe School on the right this car
goes, and then runs for a mile through streets with
giant elms forming walls on either side, or arches
overhead. Then the car comes out into open country,
with granite outcrops on the hills, while the slopes
are covered with green, and between them are meadows with waves of grass on their surfaces. At Lake
Shore avenue the Gloucester branch of the Boston &
Maine Railroad is crossed and then the car goes rush-
ing along a pretty country road where the wild flowers brush the running-boards, and past well-kept farmhouses, to come to Turtle Hill Park, with its observatory on a rocky hill at the right.

Close to the woods, laden with the fragrance of
their pine carpet, the car runs on and through Mont-
serrat, a little summer settlement, to cross an arm of
Longham meadow, with rocky Bald Hill rising on the
right. Passing Thompson's Corner the traveler goes
through the town of Wenham for a few minutes and
then enters Hamilton. Going by Four Corners, at
Woodbury's Crossing the railroad is again crossed,
and then the car climbs a series of low hills, only to
dash down again. Whether the hills be green with
the fresh grass of spring, or sere in autumn, they are
always beautiful, patches of running hemlock dotting
the green or brown. At Crooked Lane Hill a branch
line runs off to the northward to

IPSWICH. The ride is through a pretty farming country, and coming to the old town, which was
settled in 1633, after the Penobscot Indians had laid
waste the Indian village which stood there, the car

crosses Ipswich River. The town site was purchased for $100 by John Winthrop. Steamers run from here to Newbury, and plans are under way for the construction of an electric line through the town of Rowley on to connect with Newburyport, Haverhill and Lawrence.

Continuing from Crooked Lane Hill on the main line, the Gloucester car passes the town line into Essex, with Chebacco Lake, a popular resort for fishermen, off to the right. At Centennial Grove Junction a line runs off to the right to the Grove, where convenient picnic grounds are to be found. Then the car goes on to enter

ESSEX FALLS, one of the most charming rural villages in all New England. After passing the power house of the electric railway company, on the right, the car comes to a picturesque old stone bridge over a little stream, while there is a ford above the bridge, through which horses may be driven to be watered. The car runs along Martin street into Essex, which has a handsome Town Hall and Library Building, the gift of the late T. O. H. P. Burnham of Boston, who once kept the Old South Bookstore. The town also has many pretty summer houses of wealthy Bostonians.

Coming over the hills of Essex, the salt breezes blow in from the ocean, across the marshes which stretch away along the Essex River. Here is an old shipyard, and the car crosses the river near it, entering South Essex. After leaving this little summer hamlet, the car goes for some distance through fragrant pine woods, with an occasional farmhouse in view. Crossing a purling little stream, it then runs through a gigantic granite gateway which seems as though it might have been made by nature for this purpose, and comes through Slough Hill, entering West Gloucester.

From here the car goes up hill and down dale, whisking in and out of the woods, and finally coming out upon a hillside, from which one may have a charming glimpse of Annisquam, off to the left, across the 'Squam River. After going under the tracks of the railroad, and coming through another pine grove, there is a fine view of the rocky islands in the river. At Fernwood Lake, another collection of summer cottages, the road running off to Fernwood is seen at the right, and coming out upon the top of the hill and all the way down a long grade, there is a splendid view of Annisquam and Gloucester ahead. The car enters

GLOUCESTER, over the arms of the 'Squam River, which makes Cape Ann an island at high tide, Rocky Neck, Ten-Pound Island and Eastern Point, with their lighthouses are off to the right, in Gloucester Harbor, and on the left is the river, with schooners from the Annisquam fishing fleet. Below the great hotel on the right the surf beats ceaselessly on the sands. Entering the heart of the city the car stops at the street railway station where a change is made for the lines running along the north and south shores of the cape. Gloucester is the most famous fishing port in the world, and has been a fishing village since 1625. The fishing wharves and "flakes," where fish are dried, are worth a visit. A street car line runs from the station to Rocky Neck, a popular resort.

Another branch line to Long Beach is a favorite

trip for North Shore summer residents and excursionists. Running out of the quaint old town one comes to a beautiful sandy beach, where are found, in addition to sea bathing, a pavilion and dancing hall, bowling alleys and other popular attractions. Only a short distance from the sandy beach is a bold and rocky shore, and the sea views are charming, especially in the direction of Thatcher's Island and its lighthouses.

The line along the north side of the cape runs

SUNSET FROM BAY.

through the pretty summer village of Riverdale to Annisquam with its handsome villas, and on to Bay View, with seaside cottages on one side and granite quarries on the other, and then on to the terminus at Lanesville, from the hills of which there are fine views of the northern Essex and New Hampshire coasts.

From Lanesville, by taking a walk of a mile, one may come to Pigeon Cove, from which the return to Gloucester may be made on the electric line of the other side of the Cape.

Taking the Pigeon Cove and Rockport trip, the

car for Rockport soon gets out of the town, after running around some weather-beaten streets, and then goes through reaches of delightful rural scenery. At Beaver Dam a stone barn built in 1832 is passed on the left, and then the car climbs Baitcut Hill. From the standpipe on the top of this a magnificent ocean view is obtained, this point of vantage affording an opportunity to see even the South Shore as far as Plymouth. Descending the hill, Cape Pond Grove, a popular picnic ground, is seen on the right as the car comes into

VIEW AT ROCKPORT.

ROCKPORT, it runs by quaint old houses, which have the look of weather-beaten old salts, but which stand next door to modern summer cottages. Indeed, some of these old houses are the summer residences of wealthy people who prefer the picturesque to the modern. Entering the town, on the left is a Memorial Hall, and the cars, before starting on their journey to Pigeon Cove, make a complete circuit of the business part of the town, passing the ruins of a cotton mill destroyed by fire some years ago.

PIGEON COVE is reached by one of the finest electric car rides to be had anywhere. The line follows Granite street, on the left being the granite quarries for which Cape Ann is noted, and from the car

)ne occasionally gets glimpses of great chasms from
vhich the stone has been taken for years. On the
ight, as the electric line makes a wide semi-circle, are
he rolling waters of the ocean, merging from deep
)lue in the bay to a misty gray on the outer rim of the
vorld. Far out may be seen that terrible trap in the
)pen sea known as the Salvages, and although the
vater below the car may be calm, a faint sound from
cross the deep may be heard as the surf strikes on the
ocks which have wrecked more than one vessel in
ight of home.

To obtain the best view of the ocean, one should
limb Pigeon Hill, at the end of the car line. The hill,
o the left, is more than 200 feet above the level of the
ea, and from the summit parts of the coast line of
hree states may be seen distinctly. To the south
s the North Shore, and with a glass, the outline of
he South Shore may be made out. Northward is the
Jew Hampshire coast and the Isle of Shoals, and be-
'ond may be seen the mountainous coast of Maine.
\head, the ocean view is truly magnificent, and the
iext land that is to be seen by one who voyages east-
vard beyond Straitsmouth Island and Thatcher's Is-
and, with their lights, is the coast of England.

On the South Shore by Trolley.

A LONG the " South Shore," as that part of Mass-
sachusetts Bay south of Boston Harbor is
called, is a country which is much frequented
by trolley excursionists. In this section of the historic Commonwealth are great parks, beautiful drives
and walks, long sandy beaches, salt marshes, lakes,
rivers and groves, and a succession of delightful villages, with ever-changing charms of landscape. One
may travel all day with pleasure on the electric cars
which run from Boston and Quincy through the beautiful South Shore towns, to quaint, historic Bridgewater and beyond. Starting from Boston the Neponset car is taken to the Neponset River, which is the
most attractive tidal stream near Boston, with no
smoky factories or disagreeable mud flats lining its
banks, but an overhanging growth of marsh grass
reaching down to the water. Here a change is made
to the cars of the Quincy & Boston Street Railway,
and crossing the river, which is seen meandering
along from the foot of the distant hills on the right,
the car runs on to Atlantic, where a summer line of
street cars runs off to the left, to

SQUANTUM, a point much visited by excursionists, with picnic grounds and delightful marine

PETER BUTLER HOME.

views. Here it was that Miles Standish landed in the year 1621, and held council with the Indian sachem Chickatawbut. On the main line the car continues on through Norfolk Downs, the Massachusetts Fields of olden time and rides past the park in Wollaston, just beyond which is the Peter Butler house, once the residence of the Black, Greenleaf and Butler families of Quincy. Passing under the shadow of Wollaston Heights, as they rise on the left, and which were once part of the grant to William Hutchinson, the car enters the interesting city of

QUINCY, known all the world over for its granite, and closely linked to the history of our country. Before entering the Granite City one sees the famous quarries from which the stone goes to all the states in the Union, and even to foreign countries. On the ride

ADAMS ACADEMY.

one passes the homestead of Charles Francis Adams,
who was minister to England in the trying times
of the Civil War.   Adams Academy, seen on the
right, was founded in 1823, by gift of President John
Adams, and was opened for pupils in 1872.   On the
site of this building John Hancock was born.   Quincy
Square, which is soon reached contains many objects

of interest, among which
are a granite drinking
fountain, a stone Town
Hall and the First Unitarian Church, with massive
granite pillars.   Under
this church lie the re-
mains of John Adams,
second president of the
United States, and of
John Quincy Adams, the
sixth president, with those
of their wives.   The homes
of the two presidents, now
under the care of patri-
otic societies, are only a
short distance away, on

FIRST UNITARIAN CHURCH.

the road to Braintree.

Before continuing on the South Shore trip, one
may well make the interesting short trip to East Milton, to see the granite country.   The cars run for a
short distance on the trunk line to Braintree, turning
to the right at Franklin and Water streets, and crossing the railroad at Quincy Adams station, not far
from the Adams houses.   At Brewer's Corner the
granite district is entered.   Here the great ledges of
the splendid gray stone rise on every hand, with

houses perched precariously among the rocks. Two commodious brick schoolhouses, the Willard and the Gridley Bryant Schools, look quite out of place with such masses of granite around them. Soon the car turns to the north and after crossing the railroad tracks, all the way to East Milton may be seen the great quarries on the hillsides, while enormous derricks stretch their great arms on all sides. The railroad track beside which the cars run is built upon the road-bed of the first railroad in the United States, and the stone posts of the present railroad fence were once ties of the first railroad, upon which the original flat iron rails were laid. The railroad was built to carry stone from the quarries to the Neponset River when Solomon Willard, the architect of

A TYPICAL QUARRY.

Bunker Hill Monument, decided to use Quincy granite for the building material. If the traveler stops for half an hour at East Milton, and walks a little distance down the railroad track, he may see a short section of the original road, with its granite ties in position, on what was then a turnout. An appropriate bronze tablet marks the historic spot among the famous quarries.

Resuming the South Shore journey to visit Nantasket Beach, which is well worth another side trip, a car which runs through without change may be taken at Quincy Square, unless the passenger has taken the Nantasket car at Neponset, in which case no change is necessary. The Square is an important street railway junction, for beside the lines to East Milton, Squantum and Nantasket Beach, there are lines to Braintree, South Quincy, West Quincy and Hough's Neck, a popular summer resort, the different rides affording many contrasts and combinations of scenery. The Nantasket car passes out Washington street, through Quincy Point, formerly an important shipbuilding place, where many noble vessels were launched in the early part of the century. Crossing Weymouth Fore River, the car stops for a moment at New Downer Landing, formerly called Lovell's Grove, famed as a summer excursion resort. Beyond this is

NORTH WEYMOUTH, formerly "Old Spain," where the cars of the Quincy & Boston connect with those of the Hingham Street Railway Company, and until Hingham is reached, run over the state highway. "Old Spain" was the first settlement in the Commonwealth after Plymouth, and still has its original boundaries. It was founded by the buccaneer Weston in 1622. Soon after leaving the town the cars cross Weymouth Back River, so-called to distinguish it from "Fore" River, which was crossed in Quincy, and then run through a pretty wooded district belonging to the Peter Bradley estate. Off to the left a line runs to Fort Point and to the Bradley Fertilizer Works. Just before entering

HINGHAM, the camp grounds of the First Corps of Cadets may be seen on the left, and also the home of Hon. John D. Long, Secretary of the Navy. Be-

RESIDENCE OF JOHN D. LONG, SECRETARY OF THE NAVY.

fore arriving at the Hingham station, the Lincoln House, once the home of General Benjamin Lincoln, of the Revolutionary Army, may be seen on the right.

THE HOME OF GEN. BENJ. LINCOLN.

Hingham is one of the quaintest of old towns—"another Cranford," Mrs. Leslie called it. A short distance out of Hingham, the car ascends a hill from

which there is a charming unobstructed view of Hingham harbor, and the surrounding country.   From
here the car runs swiftly through the beautiful Old

THE OLD SHIP.

Colony Woods, which cannot be excelled for sylvan
scenery, to come out at

NANTASKET, one of the finest sand beaches in
the country, soon to be put under state care, and

NANTASKET BEACH.

where there are attractions enough to suit the tastes
of anyone.   Merry-go-rounds, roller-coasters, the
chutes, a dancing pavilion, bowling alleys, shooting

galleries and other devices for entertainment furnish
recreation, while the walks on the hard sands, the rest-
less surf, the open Atlantic, the rocks at the southern
extremity of the beach with their varied marine life,
and the splendid sea views, give pleasure to those of
more quiet tastes. There are several good hotels at
the beach. An electric line runs up the long neck of
land, with glimpses of the water on both sides, to

VIEW ON THE MONATIQUOT, BRAINTREE

Point Allerton and Hull. At Nantasket steamers may
be taken for Boston and carriages secured for a drive
along the famous Jerusalem Road, where many
wealthy Boston people have their summer homes.
The famous drive extends along the shore for nearly
three miles, affording the traveler many beautiful
views of the ocean, and a constant succession of fine
architectural examples.

On the return journey by electric car one may go
back by the same route as far as Hingham, and then

take a car for East Weymouth, where connections
may be made for Weymouth, Braintree, South Weymouth, Rockland, Brockton, Whitman, East Bridgewater and Bridgewater. Between Weymouth and
North Weymouth is an eminence known as King Oak
Hill, which was crowned by a giant oak until a few
years ago, and it is said that the first settlers of Weymouth camped beneath its branches and gave the tree

and the hill their names. In Weymouth is the famous
Arnold Tavern, where the Committee of Safety met
in Revolutionary times. Weymouth, South Weymouth and East Weymouth are full of historic old
houses and the trolleys run through a succession of
fine places. They also pass the largest boulder in
eastern Massachusetts, House Rock. The locality
is a famous one for the sportsmen who fish or shoot
ducks.

Running southward from Hingham, on the main line of the journey, the ride is to

HINGHAM CENTRE, over one of the finest streets in the world, nearly 200 feet wide, and lined on either side by double rows of giant elms. The car passes to the right of a meeting house erected in 1681, and said to be the oldest house of worship in the

HARTSUFF PARK.

United States in use at the present day. Leaving this beautiful thoroughfare, through Hingham Centre, the car passes through a rural district to South Hingham, and then to the old turnpike at

QUEEN ANN'S CORNER, near which once dwelt three maiden sisters who remained loyal to the king through two wars and who claimed George IV as their sovereign fifty years after the Declaration of Independence was signed. Near Queen Anne's Corner is Accord Pond, which takes its name from the

happy "accord" between the parties to an old contract.
When a treaty with the Indians was to be made by the
towns of Scituate, Abington and Hingham, the parties
decided to meet at the junction of the boundaries of
the three towns. As this was near the centre of the
pond, the meeting was held on the ice, and an amica-
ble settlement was made, after which the pond was

given its present name. From Queen Anne's Corner
the car continues on to North Hanover, a town which
dates back to 1633, and a line leads to Assinippi,
which, as its Indian name indicates, is "a place of
rocks and water," once a famous shipping mart. Running southwest to

ROCKLAND, (East Abington) the car goes on
wide, shaded streets which branch from Lane's Corner. After leaving Rockland the street soon crosses
the Plymouth line of the New York, New Haven &
Hartford Railroad, and after a run through country

scenery, where leafy groves alternate with open fields and pastures, the town of

WHITMAN is entered. This is a busy shoe manufacturing town, from which street railway lines run to Brockton on the west and northward to Abington and North Abington. It is also a historic town,. from which came planks for the Frigate "Constitution," and where was cast the first church bell in the Colony, by Col. Aaron Hobart, who taught Paul Revere the art. From Whitman the journey is southward through a rural country to

EAST BRIDGEWATER. This is a growing and prosperous village, with several churches and varied manufactures. Here are fine old houses and the Washburn Library, the gift of Cyrus Washburn. Sachem Rock, Robins Pond and Matfield River afford many picturesque views. It is only a short ride from here to

BRIDGEWATER, an historic town, with many manufactures. The town, a part of the Indian domain of Nunketest, was bought, soon after the landing of the Pilgrims, of the Indian chief Massasoit, and was named Bridgewater in 1645, after the town in old Somersetshire. Colonial records state that the transaction was made between the Indians and Myles Standish, Samuel Nash and Constant Southworth, and that the payment for this magnificent domain was seven coats, one and one-half yards to a coat, nine hatchets, eight hoes, twenty knives, four moose skins, and ten and one-half yards of cotton. It was in this town that Hugh Orr erected a trip-hammer, and in 1748 made 500 muskets, the first turned out in America, for the province of Massachusetts. In the Revolution he made many brass and iron cannon and cannon balls for the Continental Army. The old forge of Orr was on the Matfield River. From Bridgewater direct connection may be made with Taunton, or the traveller may return to Boston by going to Brockton and from there to Quincy via Holbrook or Randolph, reversing a part of the route given elsewhere, under "Into the Old Colony."

Mercantile Trust Co.

WATER STREET, CORNER OF CONGRESS
BOSTON, MASS.

OFFICERS :

JOSIAH Q. BENNETT, *Presiaent.*

ANDREW W. PRESTON, *Vice-Prest.*   J. E. GILCREAST, *Treas.*

F. T. MONROE, *Secretary.*

**Interest Paid on Deposits Subject to Check.
Corporation, Firm, Individual and Trust Accounts Solicited.
Acts as Trustee under Wills or Otherwise.
A General Banking Business Transacted.**

DIRECTORS:

JOSIAH Q. BENNETT,	A. W. PRESTON.	SUMNER C. STANLEY.
DENMAN BLANCHARD.	HARRY E. RUSSELL.	HALES W. SUTER.
S. S. BLANCHARD.	SAMUEL SHAW.	ABNER J. TOWER.
A. N. BURBANK.	ALFRED A. GLAZIER.	H. O. UNDERWOOD.
D. H. COOLIDGE.	C. S. HAPGOOD.	H. D. YERXA.
LIVINGSTON CUSHING.	ROBERT F. HERRICK.	WM. A. RUSSELL.
NEIL MCNEIL.	C. A. HOPKINS.	SIMON DAVIS.
N. C. NASH.	CHARLES L. JAMES.	HERBERT H. WHITE.

Into the Old Colony.

ONE of the grand trunk lines of electric railway southward from Boston runs through the "Old Colony" and the cities of Quincy, Brockton, Taunton and Fall River to Newport, New Bedford or Providence. The Boston Elevated Railway car is taken to Neponset, where a change is made to the Quincy and Boston line running to Quincy by the route described elsewhere. When paying the fare on the Quincy car, an eight-cent check to the South Braintree line may be obtained. Changing at Quincy Square to the car marked Braintree and Holbrook, a short ride brings one to the corner of Franklin Street and Independence Avenue.

On the right are two old weather-beaten houses, one the birthplace of President John Adams, and the other the birthplace of President John Quincy Adams. The front door of the home of the elder Adams looks directly upon the end of the John Quincy Adams house. The John Adams place is occupied by the widow of a soldier, and is cared for by Adams Chapter, Daughters of the American Revolution. A fine view of West Quincy and its granite quarries is had as the car runs on into

BRAINTREE, with its granite quarries, its shoe factories and general business, surrounded by a rich agricultural country. Here is the famous "trilobite quarry" known to geologists. Cars may be taken here for Weymouth, East Braintree, Hingham and Nantasket Beach. Passing through the town without change, the car comes to

SOUTH BRAINTREE, passing Thayer Academy on the right, the gift to the town of General Sylvanus Thayer, who left $200,000 for this purpose. From here there are two lines to Brockton. One

BIRTHPLACE OF JOHN ADAMS AND JOHN QUINCY ADAMS.

passes through Holbrook and Brookville, the former a shoe manufacturing town, with a Gothic Town Hall and Public Library, the handsome Winthrop Church, and many fine estates, notable among which is the Adams place. From Brookville there is a good view of the surrounding country. Then the line runs into Montello, where connections are made with the Brockton, Bridgewater & Taunton Street Railway, and another ride of fifteen minutes takes the passenger to Brockton, going past Brockton Common and the shoe factories.

The other line from South Braintree goes through Randolph. Changing to a Randolph car, the traveler goes by the cemetery on the left, and then by Stanwood Grove, a favorite place for picnics. Running past fine farms and farm residences, the car reaches Central Square,

RANDOLPH, where are located the Turner Library, the Town Hall, the Congregational Church and the Howard House, a famous old hostelry. Changing to the cars of the Brockton Street Railway Company, the car passes the home of Mary E. Wilkins, the famous New England writer, on the left. Crossing the line into

AVON, the car passes the handsome residences of Hiram and David Henry Blanchard, retired shoe manufacturers. Going by the Gifford School and the Pumping Station which supplies Avon with spring water, one may see a ruined windmill on the old Porter farm, and after a short run

HIGHLAND PARK is reached. This pleasure ground, which is owned by the Brockton Street Railway Company, is situated in Avon and covers about twenty-four acres. It is doubtless one of the prettiest free parks in this section of the

FOUNDATIONS OF A WINDMILL BUILT HALF A CENTURY AGO BUT NEVER COMPLETED.

ZERUBBABEL IV., A RESIDENT OF HIGHLAND PARK.

State, being laid out in a very attractive manner, with beautiful walks, luxurious beds of flowers and masses of shrubbery and comfortable shady nooks.

From the Observation Tower a very good view of the Park and surrounding country can be obtained. Among the numerous buildings located in the Park are the summer house, band stand, dancing pavilion, spring house, theatre, dining-room, etc. It is an ideal spot for picnic parties, as there is a splendid grove of chestnut trees under whose shade tables can be spread. Through the grove are scattered a large number of park swings, and plenty of seats are provided in every portion of the grounds.

Some of the amusement features are the stage attractions (a stage show being given every afternoon and evening, except Sunday, throughout the season); the band concerts, which are given every Tuesday and Thursday evenings, with a sacred concert each Sunday afternoon; the Zoo, which contains a fine collection of animals and birds, something new being introduced each season; the merry-go-round; dancing pavilion; ball grounds; mystic maze; shooting gallery, etc.

There is also an especially fine electric fountain, which is a source of constant wonder and enjoyment as its vari-colored and ever-changing streams are seen shooting upward and then falling in graceful curves to the basin below. The fact that this fountain cost nearly $6000.00 will show that it is an exceptionally fine one.

One of the features of the Zoo is the famous bear "Zerubbabel," who came into public notice by his memorable trip from 'Frisco with the Golden Gate Commandery, Knight Templars, to Boston, on the occasion of the Triennial Conclave of the Grand Encampment of Knight Templars of the United States, held in Boston in August 1895. This bear was captured, when a cub, in the mountains near San Francisco by a member of the Golden Gate Commandery, and taken by them as a mascot on this trip. He was formally presented to the Bay State Commandery of Brockton, August 29, 1895, by the Golden Gate Commandery, while on a visit to that city. Zerubbabel makes the Park his home the year around, taking his long winter's nap there, and is always ready to welcome the summer visitors at the Park, and to eat the peanuts and candy with which the children delight to feed him. The dining room is well equipped, and parties can be sure of finding there a plentiful supply of food, fruits, ice cream, and tonics, and at reasonable prices. The admission to the grounds is absolutely free. Small charges are made for the use of the merry-go-round, dancing pavilion and shooting gallery, and, of course, at the dining pavilion, but everything else is free.

Amateur photographers will find at the Park an opportunity for taking quite a number of very fine pictures of various portions of the grounds and some of the buildings. The animals in the Zoo would also make interesting subjects. Soon after leaving here the car passes the residence of Harvey Crawford on the left, with its great greenhouses, and reaching the junction where the Holbrook car enters

BROCKTON, a fine view is had of the Douglas Shoe Factories off to the left. Like Lynn, Brockton is a great "shoe town," sending its manufactures all over the civilized world. Along Main street the car passes · the homes of many wealthy business men. Going by the Winthrop School and Ashland Cemetery, the car passes the Commercial Club house on the right, at Main and Spring streets, and then the car reaches Brockton Common, or Perkins Park, a centre for the many street railway lines entering the town.

Radiating from here are four lines of railway to neighboring towns, one of them connecting with Abington, North Abington and other places in the South Shore Country. Another line runs through a beautiful farming country, past a pretty pond, into the village of

NORTH EASTON, where, in the great Ames factories, three-fifths of all the shovels made in the world are turned out. The town was the home of the late H. H. Richardson, who gave a new and distinctive stamp to American architecture, and it contains many beautiful specimens of his work. The handsome private estates of the Ameses are among the finest country places in the United States, and through the liberality of this family, the town has a beautiful High School, which, with the railroad station and the beautiful Memorial Church of the Unitarians are architectural models. From North Easton cars connect with Norton, Mansfield and Attleboro. Another line from Brockton runs to

STOUGHTON, penetrating an agricultural dis-rict, this important shoe-making town, lying up mong the hills, from some of which beautiful vistas of ountry can be seen. Still another Brockton line di-erges to

WHITMAN, another shoe town, from which a trect railway line connects with Abington and other laces along the South Shore Country. There are .vo ways of reaching Taunton from Brockton. The 1ost direct route is by way of the Taunton & Brockton treet Railway line, which runs from Brockton south-'ard over the old Boston and Taunton turnpike.

The scenery is of an attractive character, the ountry views varying at every turn. The route leads 1rough the western part of Bridgewater township, 'ith its delightful scenery, and then runs through the illage of Cochesset, in one place crossing an extensive wamp on a trestle bridge which is more than a mile)ng, and is a notable piece of electric railway engi-eering. Entering the town of Raynham, a short run rings the passenger to

NORTH RAYNHAM, where the tracks of the ew York, New Haven & Hartford Railroad are panned by a splendid steel trestle. From here it is nly a short distance into Taunton. The other line ·om Brockton to Taunton runs through the suburb f Campello. passing the handsome residences of 'oses Packard and George E. Keith. Here a change ; made to the cars of the Brockton, Bridgewater & 'aunton Street Railway, which run past the homes of ictory workers, and then a country of market gar-ens and farms before coming to

WEST BRIDGEWATER. The Female Seminary is passed on the left before reaching the Soldiers' Monument and West Bridgewater Square. Crossing the Taunton River, and running through open country past the street railway power station, a good view is had of the great Bridgewater standpipe, before entering

VIEW ON THE TAUTNON RIVER NEAR TAUNTON.

BRIDGEWATER, where connection is made by the electric railway with the towns of the South Shore. Going through the little village of Scotland, the next point of interest is Nippenicket Lake on the right, with its two pretty parks, Nippenicket and Pilgrim, the latter being controlled by the street railway company. This was an Indian camping ground and arrow-heads and other relics are often found. Both parks have fine groves, pavilions, boathouses and other attractions.

Going on through the outskirts of Raynham the

ınton Little River is passed on the right and John-
's Pond on the left, both supplying water power
the great tack factories located there. A short
: brings one within view of the beautiful Taunton
er, which the car follows for more than a mile,
sing the clubhouse of the Taunton Boat Club be-
: coming into

TAUNTON, passing the City Hall and running
) City Square, or Taunton Green, the centre of
electric car lines which radiate from the city. The
n is noted for its manufactures, yet is clean and
tty. It has among its institutions the buildings of
State Insane Asylum. Taunton was founded by
ıs Elizabeth Pool, a pious Puritan of Taunton in
Somersetshire. The settlement prospered under
friendship of the Indians until 1676, when King
lip's war broke out. Led by the son of Massasoit,
Indians attacked the place, but were repulsed, and
vas from Taunton that was led the expedition
ch pursued the Indians until King Philip was
ed.
Of the monuments of the present in Taunton, few
 more imposing than the Bristol County Court
use, a magnificent gray stone building, located on
ınton Green, where are also the Post Office and
 City Hotel. Here also is the first Unitarian
ırch, a rambling stone structure with Saxon
ers. One of the great industries of Taunton is the
ınton Locomotive Works.
Most of the points of interest in Taunton can be
ı by taking journeys on the lines of the Taunton
:et Railway. One branch runs to Brittaniaville or
.ittenville, noted for its great silver-plating estab-

lishments and manufactories of table ware. Another goes to Prospect Hill, Scadding Pond or Weir (pronounced "Ware"), village, where twenty tons of iron are used daily in the manufacture of stoves by one company. Here was established the first bloomer iron furnace in New England, in 1656.

Perhaps the most popular line of the Taunton Street Railway is that to Sabbatia Park, which was laid out and equipped by the company. The park occupies a delightful site upon the side of Sabbatia Lake,

SABBATIA PARK.

and is provided with a handsome grove, with rustic seats, swings, pavilions, tables, and everything for the entertainment of picnic parties, whlie there are many devices to interest the casual pleasure seeker.

To continue the journey to Fall River and Newport, a change is made at City Square, Taunton, to the lines of the Dighton, Somerset & Swansea Street Railway. The car runs for a distance between handsome residences, and then comes to the Taunton River again as Weir Village is entered. Leaving this busy spot behind, something more of rural life is seen on the way to

NORTH DIGHTON, where a beautiful old picnic grove is passed, known to local fame as the

North Dighton Clambake Grounds. A short distance beyond is an ancient landmark, Dighton Furnace, and a paper manufactory.

With glimpses of the river the car runs on, nearing Dighton, passing the old Hodijah Baylies place, now owned by Charles Noble Simmons. Entering

DIGHTON, through the residence district, the car passes the Unitarian Church, Dighton Memorial Hall and two stove manufactories. Passing along the river, one may see three small wharves running into the river from four old houses; this was once the port of entry for Somerset, Taunton, and Troy (now Fall River) and the Custom House was in one

A SCENE ALONG THE LINE.

of these old houses. Along the line of this railway, in June, may be seen hundreds of strawberry pickers. On Assonet Neck, across the River in Berkeley, is the famous Dighton Rock, inscribed with hieroglyphics, variously credited to ancient Indians, Norsemen and Phoenicians. A ride of forty-five minutes from Taunton brings one to

DIGHTON ROCK PARK, owned by the Dighton, Somerset & Swansea Street Railway Company, picturesquely situated on the river bank. Between the street and the imposing main building, which is in the Moorish style of architecture, is a great lawn with planted shrubbery and carpet flower beds, gravel walks and bicycle paths.

Inside the Park are bowling alleys, a dancing hall, billiard rooms, an immense dining hall and merry-go-rounds, while on the river are steam launches and row-boats. Band concerts and entertainments are

A SCENE ALONG THE LINE.

given here on summer afternoons, and in the evening the park is brilliantly illuminated by thousands of electric lights. Adjoining the park is the fine club-house of the Taunton Boat Club. Leaving the Park, the car passes Broad Cove and climbs a hill, running through an avenue of elms into

SOMERSET, a town rich in old mansions, some of which were built fronting upon the river, when the shipping interest was paramount here. Leaving the

town, the Taunton River again comes into view, and
the hills of Fall River are seen in the distance. Soon
the car reaches Slade's Ferry Bridge, over which the
car runs into Bowenville, to take cars of the Globe
Street Railway Company, which land them at City
Hall.

FALL RIVER, passing the magnificent station
of the New York, New Haven & Hartford Railroad,
the Court House, the Armory, the Young Men's
Christian Association, the handsome stone Public
Library and the City Hall. From Fall River electric
lines radiate east and south to New Bedford and
Newport, respectively.

The line from Fall River to New Bedford and
Fairhaven runs through Westport Factory, Lincoln
Park and North Dartmouth. Lincoln Park is mid-
way between Fall River and New Bedford, and is an
attractive place, leased to the street railway company.
Continuing on the main journey by electric car from
Fall River to.Newport, there are bits of scenery which
are distinctively American; then comes a corner
which suggests old England, and here and there is
seen a whirling windmill which reminds the traveler
of Holland. The delights of the artist-traveler will
be unbounded on this trip, especially if he makes it
in autumn, when the country is at its best. The island
part of Rhode Island was known to the Indians as
Aquidneck, "Floating on the Water." The name
of Rhode Island itself is said by some to be derived
from Rood Eylandt or Red Island, given it by a
party of Hollanders who first saw it when its forests
were tinged with the autumnal crimson. But while
it is seen at its best when its verdure has just been

touched by the early frosts, it is always beautiful, and the ride to the "Queen of Watering Places" is one of the most enjoyable to be found in New England.

Starting from Fall River, the "Border City," which was once partly in Rhode Island, the cars of the Newport & Fall River Electric Railway run for a short distance through the cotton mill district, which is the largest textile industries centre in the

POST TAVERN, TIVERTON

world, and leaves the mills at the state line to enter the picturesque and historic town of

TIVERTON. In the early days this town had its share of the Indian fighting, and here the seven Church brothers started their menhaden fisheries, which caught fish from the sea all the way from Canada to Cape Hatteras. Later, the fishermen became whalers, and sailed around Cape Horn to the Pacific seas. The great sight of Tiverton, however, is the Stone

Bridge, which was erected some nine years ago, and considered by Tivertonians, the eighth wonder of the world. It divides the towns of Tiverton and Portsmouth, and is the only means of reaching the island part of Rhode Island, except by boat. Below the heights, near the bridge, is the new Island Park, over which blow the fresh breezes, salt laden, from the Seaconnet. Leaving the water and turning to the left, the car enters

VIEW FROM STONE BRIDGE.

NEWTOWN, where Ann Hutchinson settled with her followers. From here the journey is southward along a country road, walled in by boulders and shaded by great trees, passing now and then a delightful old farmhouse, with its well-sweep and "old oaken bucket." Near here is the Glen, the private estate of Henry A. C. Taylor, with its little church in which Dr. Channing, the great apostle of Unitarianism, once preached. On the right is Lawton's Valley, rich in trees and verdure, watered by a small stream flowing eastward. Then the car begins to ascend the slopes of Quaker Hill, the view from which is of surpassing beauty. Looking backward, the hills of Fall River may be seen, while Tiverton appears in the near distance of the valley below. The farms around are blocked out by stone walls. Off to the right the Providence River rises and falls with the tide, and on the left can be seen the East River, or East Passage, with a white-sailed yacht shining on its blue surface. Ahead is

PORTSMOUTH VILLAGE, and through this the car runs on its way to Newport. In Portsmouth, Coddington and his friends established the settlement of Pocasset before moving on to Newport. It is hard to realize that this little village, in which the most prominent point of interest is now the Town Hall, was once the seat of the General Assembly of Rhode Island, sharing the honor with Providence, Newport and Warwick. There are enchanting views in all this portion of the journey. The river flows smoothly in the valley below, and on either hand rise the hills, dotted by comfortable farmhouses. A short distance beyond the town is the Vanderbilt farm, or "Oakland Farm," as it is called, which was once owned by August Belmont, and on which stood the Terfey Tea House, some ten years ago moved to a location nearer Newport. Passing the great farm the car soon comes to St. Mary's Church on the right, in memory of Raymond Belmont, half hidden behind stately pines. The old stone church, with its peaceful burying ground, is well worth a visit. Passing the Terfey Tea House, leaving the farming country, and crossing the line into

MIDDLETOWN, the traveler is in the only town in the state without a village or a postoffice. Here a final glimpse is had of the East Passage, on the left, and a panoramic succession of hills and dales is presented. Beyond the Middletown line, after a pleasant run between more farms, the car passes to the right of the famous Brier Tea House, for many years the scene of festivities in which the wealth and beauty of Newport was prominent, and now often

THE OLD RHODE ISLAND WINDMILL.

visited by bicycling and coaching parties from Newport. Beyond here, any day in the year when the wind serves, one may see quaint old windmills, with all sails spread, revolving their giant arms to run the machinery which grinds out the famous Rhode Island corn meal. Seen in the dusk of evening one may imagine these windmills to be great monsters, as did Don Quixote that one against which he made his noted charge. Whirling along on the electric car, the traveler soon begins to realize that he is approaching Newport, and climbing a small eminence the watering place and the ocean are in full view. The great Vanderbilt and Gœlet mansions loom up in the distance like castles. Off to the left may be seen the quiet waters of Norman Pond, from which Newport obtains its water supply. Going down the

hill and turning off West Main road to the left, the
car makes another ascent, climbing Honeyman's
Hill from which another good view is obtained,
Coddington Cove and Coddington Point being seen
off to the right as the car enters

NEWPORT. Soon after crossing the line the
car runs between fine farms where herds of cattle
graze in one pasture, horses in another, and here and
there a flock of sheep add to the picturesque quality
of a naturally beautiful landscape. In the northerly
part of Newport the car runs to the left of Tammany
Hill, or Miantonomy Hill, as it was known in the old
days. When William Coddington and his friends
settled Newport in 1639, they found the whole island
governed by a local sachem named Wannumetonomy,
who was subject to the sachem of the Narragansetts.
He lived on this hill, to which the settlers gave the
latter part of his name, but even this abbreviation
did not suffice, and the name was shortened to
Tonomy, which a later generation corrupted to
Tammany. This hill was fighting ground in Revolutionary times, and even now may be seen remains
of the breastworks thrown up by the British under
Sir Robert Pigott. Readers of Thomas W. Higgin-
son's " Malbone : a Romance of Oldport," will be
interested to know that this land was once owned and
occupied by the family of the artist Malbone. Here
they entertained in royal style, but one day in 1766
the house was burned, the fire starting as a party of
guests were sitting down to dinner. Leaving the
hill and all its historic associations, the ride into
Newport is through varying natural scenery, the
nearer landscape being an alternation of sunny slopes,

ine groves, giant boulders, rock masses and ledges,
whie glimpses of the ocean may now and then be
cen, and on the water's edge, to the right, are views
f the United States Naval War College on Coaster's
Harbor Island. Over the bay, beyond, lies in full
iew, the village of Jamestown, on Conanicut Island.
oon the car comes to One Mile Corner, and leaving
he open country, runs into the town. As it passes
outh on Broadway, many of the handsome residences
or which Newport is famous are seen, and after
eaving Equality Park, with its fine Soldier's Monu-
ent, the car passes the Parade Grounds and Wash-
igton Park, on the right, before reaching the centre
f the city, and the terminus of one of the pleasantest
ourneys which can be made by electric car.

THE OLD STONE MILL, NEWPORT.

To the Historic Southwest.

FROM Taunton to Providence a direct line runs southwest, opening up to the traveler a section of country of great historic interest, and heretofore reached only with some difficulty. The line runs through the villages of Westville, Annawan Rock, Rehoboth, Seekonk and East Providence, and every mile of the journey is over historic ground. Here it was that the battles of King Philip's war were fought to the death, and in this lovely spot, in 1636, the hermit Blackstone settled, having left the "tyranny of the lords-brethren." The Reverend Samuel Newman, who led here a little flock from Weymouth, found the eccentric Blackstone in possession, but there was room in Rehoboth for them all, as nearly all the territory covered by this new electric line was then in that town.

Starting from Taunton, where it connects with electric lines from Boston, Brockton and elsewhere, the Providence & Taunton line runs to the southwest, soon leaving the city behind, and entering a beautiful rural country in the corner of the town of Dighton. The car soon passes on the left, the famous Annawan Rock, in Squannakonk swamp, where Captain Benjamin Church captured Annawan, the last leader of King Philip's warriors, who was beheaded at Boston, in spite of the promise of Captain

Church that his life should be spared, and in the
face of the protests of his captor. About a mile
farther on, the car passes, on the right, the Annawan
Hotel, known as the half-way house from Providence
to Taunton. The town of

REHOBOTH, in which the traveler now finds
himself, has an interesting history. It was once the
rival of Boston for the honor of being the capital
city of Massachusetts, and was defeated by only a
few votes. Broken-hearted, it settled down into a
quiet despondency, from which the electric cars are
just beginning to awaken it. On the right of the
electric line are the Baptist church and the power
house of the Providence & Taunton Street Railway
Company, the latter erected at a cost of $40,000.
Opposite the power house, shaded by a giant elm, is
the Goff Memorial Hall, on the site of the Goff
Homestead, and containing the Blanding Library,
the gift of Mr. and Mrs. Thomas W. Bicknell; a
hall for meetings, a school room, and the collections
of the Antiquarian Society. The antiquarian rooms
contain many valuable colonial relics, among which
is King Philip's kettle, and also hold the fine collection of relics from the Holy Land, the gift of Esek
H. Pierce. Beyond the postoffice on the left, where
John C. Manvel has served as postmaster for fifty-
two years, is the Congregational Church, and then
the car runs through two and one-half miles of rural
scenery, crossing the town line into

SEEKONK, and soon entering a little country
village. The car passes on the right, the new town
hall and then goes by the great Hopkins Stock Farm,

known locally as the " Potter Place." The handsome
residence of Mrs. Amy Potter, wife of E. H. Potter
and daughter of the late W. H. Hopkins, is one of
the places of interest, and the barns where stock of
high pedigree is kept are seen on the left before
coming to the residence. Across the way are the
stables of Mr. Potter, where many fine horses are
kept and trained. The stock farm is near the East
Providence line, which is also the state boundary between Massachusetts and Rhode Island, and the car
approaches the town after crossing a meadow, and
runs beside a brook which is a favorite haunt for
artists. This town is where the Newman Church
settlement was made, and it was one of those villages
which suffered by fire in the Indian wars. Crossing
the narrow township, the traveler comes within sight
of the long arm of Providence River coming down to
meet the swelling tide. Crossing this stretch of
flowing water, the terminus of the line is reached, in
Providence, where connections may be made with
the various city street railway lines. Along most of
the route the scenery is distinctively rural in character, with views of fertile farms, shady groves,
tangled wildernesses and wide-spreading meadows.

A Journey Inland by Trolley.

—

ONE may now ride from Boston westward to Worcester and from there to Fitchburg, by one of the great trunk lines of electric railway which penetrates the "Heart of the Commonwealth." From the Subway the ride is by the Newton Boulevard and Commonwealth avenue cars as far as Washington street in Newton, by the route taken in going to Norumbega Park, which may well be visited before continuing on the Worcester trip. At Washington street a change is made to the Wellesley & Boston Street Railway cars, going past the Woodland Park Hotel, over the Boston & Albany tracks and by the Newton Cottage Hospital before coming to

NEWTON LOWER FALLS. The terminus is at the bridge, below which are the falls, the water power being used to run the woolen factory on the right. Changing to the cars of the Natick & Cochituate Street Railway, the ride is along Washington street to

WELLESLEY HILLS. Between handsome elms the car runs past Elm Park Hotel on the right and the Wellesley High School on the left. Following the railway line, which goes through a deep cut in the rocks, and going through an open country, the car runs into

WELLESLEY, the Town Hall and Public Library being seen on an eminence to the right. These were a gift to the town by Hollis Hunnewell, whose beautiful place is one of the features of Wellesley, and at Wellesley Square carriages meet those who wish to visit the fine estate, reached after a fifteen-minute ride. From here a line runs to Needham where connections are made with cars for various parts described elsewhere. Resuming the journey at the Square the cars turn into Central street, and reaching Blossom street the first view is had of Wellesley College, off to the left, the spires the buildings being seen above the trees. The car runs for a mile along the college grounds, passing West Stone Lodge, one of the entrances. On the right Morse's Pond is seen, and on the left lovely Lake Waban, where the college girls row. At the bridge between the two lakes, known as Wellesley Lakes Station, Pond street passes off to the left, between the college grounds and the Hunnewell estate, past which the car runs for some distance before entering

NATICK. This old town, devoted to the making of shoes, was where Henry Wilson, afterwards vice-president, served an apprenticeship at the shoe-maker's bench. Transfers may be made here for Felchville, North Natick and Cochituate, and South Natick. The last named is an historic town on the Charles River. The ride is a short and pleasant one, over a hill which gives a wide view of the upper Charles River valley. The terminus is near Bailey's

Hotel, a famous old tavern. This town was where John Eliot had his Christian Indian village, and where he translated the Bible into Indian language. The only monument to his memory is a giant elm under which he used to preach. South Natick is the original Oldtown of Harriet Beecher Stowe's "Oldtown Folks."

From Natick there are two lines to South Framingham. One is by way of Saxonville, while the more direct route is by the South Middlesex car, taken at Natick Common. A walk to the left brings one to this car, near the Natick Soldiers' Monument. A few steps away, on Central street, is the old Wilson house. Across the Common is the Morse Public Library. After leaving Natick the car passes the site of the Indian Burying Ground, on the right, then Dug Pond and the reservoir of the Natick Water Works, and then crosses an arm of Lake Cochituate. Dell Park Cemetery is passed, and ascending Hogan's Hill there is a fine view of Natick, and in the distance on the left, is the State Reformatory for Women at Sherborne. Following the railroad tracks and crossing Beaver Dam brook, South Framingham is entered.

The Natick & Cochituate car for Saxonville starts from the railroad station in Natick. Crossing the railroad and going along Main street it comes in sight of Lake Cochituate on the left, and then passes, on the same side, the Sunnyside Trotting Park. Through Felchville the car runs into the little village of

COCHITUATE, thence past farms until Dudley Pond, on the right, with its fine grove, is reached. A little further on, from the hilltop, a splendid view is had of the lake, its banks shaded by tall trees, and its

inlets running up into the meadows. Continuing on,
the car passes to the left of the home of the Reverend
Father Murphy, founder of the John Boyle O'Reilly
Band. Among the attractions of the place is a mena-
gerie. Running down the hill the car line terminates
at the railroad tracks in

SAXONVILLE. From here the Framingham
Union Street Railway operates a line to South Framingham, recently changed from a horse-car line to an
electric. The first point of interest is Wayside Park,
on the left, with its pretty pine and chestnut grove,
baseball grounds and bicycle track. This is also a
popular resort for picnic parties, provided with all the
necessary buildings for the accommodation of those
seeking a day's outing. Farms, with their crops and
cattle, are passed after leaving Wayside Park, and a
short run brings one to the State Militia Grounds on
the right. Here, if the visitor goes when the Massachusetts Volunteer Militia is in camp, he will see long
rows of white tents, the gay life of the military canton-
ment, and the Stars and Stripes floating from the top
of a tall flagstaff. As the car enters South Framingham, residences and business blocks are passed, and
the terminus is reached at the railroad crossing.

From South Framingham there is a branch line
to Ashland and Hopkinton, via the South Middlesex
Street Railway. The car passes manufacturing plants,
and on the right the handsome Nevins estate on the
Sudbury River. Going through Ashland, and passing Green Meadow Farm, the car enters Hopkinton.
Here the Poor Farm buildings are passed on the right,
and at the top of Meeting House Hill is the historic
stone Claflin-Valentine house, said to be two hundred

years old. The car passes the Public Library and Post Office in Hopkinton Centre.

Another branch line from South Framingham reaches Milford and Hopedale. The car passes Lake Waushakum on the right, and about two miles out of town goes up Whitney's Hill; after running through a rural country

EAST HOLLISTON is entered, the nail factory of Representative Talbot being seen on the left, and the Holliston Pumping Station and the street car company's power house on the right. Beyond this the line passes two elms, more than 125 years old, one measuring twenty-eight and the other thirty-two feet in circumference. On both sides are handsome residences. On Mount Hollis, on the right, signal fires warned early settlers of Indian Invasions. In Holliston the car passes the Methodist Church, an old cemetery, a Soldiers Monument, the Town Hall, and back from the road the Holliston High School. On the left are the Catholic Church and the Talbot residence. Opposite is the Congregational Church. Beyond Holliston Centre the car climbs Phillips Hill, and about two and one-half miles beyond, on the right, is a house built in 1791. Passing an old cemetery, the car enters Milford, running between the famous Milford granite quarries. From here a branch line runs off to Medway, passing through West Medway. Leaving the churches and the Town Hall of Milford, the car goes to Hopedale, the home of William H. Draper, Minister to Italy. The fine Memorial Hall in the town was given by him. Hopedale is a pretty town, with macadamized streets lined with shade trees.

SOUTH FRAMINGHAM is an important railroad centre, and its tributary electric lines contribute in no small degree to its importance. Lines run from here to Milford and Hopedale, Medway, Ashland, Hopkinton and Framingham Centre, as well as to Saxonville and Boston by the routes previously described. The route to Framingham Centre, on the way to Worcester, via the Framingham & Marlboro Electric Railway, is well shaded for the entire distance, and the scenery is of a diversified character. A short distance out of South Framingham, the car line passes the Fair Grounds on the right and Lakeview Camp Grounds on the left, where the New England Assembly of the Chautauqua meets every year in July; then climbs a hill from which is afforded a splendid view of Farm Pond, on the left. The Sudbury Aqueduct runs across this pond. Passing the fine Day place on the left, the Sudbury River itself is soon reached, and ahead can be seen the State Normal School building in

FRAMINGHAM CENTRE. The car runs to the right of Normal Hill, on which are situated the school buildings and the standpipe of the Framingham Water Works. The little village of Framingham is an interesting place, once situated on the main line of travel from Boston to New York, when it had a famous inn. The town is built around a level green, on which front the Town Hall, the old church and the Academy, founded in 1792. From Framingham Centre the road leads along the shores of one of the old basins of the Metropolitan Water System, and then past the new Sudbury Basin, officially known as No. 5, into the village of Fayville. The traveler will see much that is of interest along the route of this great water supply system, the car crossing an arm of the great basin after leaving Fayville. Then it soon goes over the bridge of the New York, New Haven & Hartford Railway, and passes the Catholic church in

SOUTHBORO. This is one of the pretty rural hill towns of Central Massachusetts and has a Soldiers' Monument in the green in front of the Congregational church. In this town, also, is the Episcopal St. Mark's School, with its handsome stone chapel. Leaving the village, the new plant of the famous Deerfoot Farm Company is passed and a quick run is made to Marlboro Junction, a short distance beyond which are the car houses of the company, nearly opposite the old Parmenter Farm. Back of this farm, on the hill, are the lands of the Chestnut Hill Association. From a hill which the car ascends, one gets a view of the factories and shops, and soon a turn brings him to Main street in the city of

MARLBORO, interesting in many ways. Here was a village of Eliot's Christian Indians, known as Okommakamesitt, and King Philip's warriors attacked the place in 1676. The modern town has much of interest, also. On the left of Main street is Holy Trinity (Episcopal) Church, presented to the parish by J. Montgomery Sears of Boston, and then comes the business district of the town. The New York, New Haven & Hartford station is on the left, and as the cars ascend the street at the farther end of the town, the new High School building is seen on the right. At the Soldiers' Monument a change is made to the cars of the Worcester & Marlboro Street Railway Company. Nearly opposite the monument is the G. A. R. Hall, in front of which hangs the original John Brown bell, captured and buried by Marlboro boys while in the army, and afterwards dug up and brought here.

Before going on to Worcester it is worth while to make a side trip to Hudson, on the branch line from Marlboro. Instead of leaving the car at the Soldiers' Monument, however, the passenger should keep on until the Fitchburg Railroad station is reached. Here a change is made to the Hudson line, on Friend Hill. Hudson is 325 feet lower than the altitude of Marlboro. and the descent is something like a toboggan slide.

After running down Mechanic street in Marlboro, a sharp turn to the left is made and the car leaves the roads, running through the fields and woods. Down the hillside it plunges, affording ever-changing views. Halfway to Hudson there is a little rise, but it is only to prepare for a second plunge down a wooded slope. Finally the car, after its cross-country run, comes out on the Northboro and Hudson road, close to the Brigham House, more than a century old. Near here is the Riverside Trotting Park. The Assabet River flows on the left, and between it and the road is Wood Park, presented to the town by Marshall Wood in 1896. A short distance beyond, the car stops in

HUDSON. This is a thriving inland Massachusetts town, and the business district, which was wiped out by a disastrous fire in 1894, has been rebuilt. From here a line will be in operation next summer connecting with the line at Clinton. The traveler

will have fifteen minutes to visit the falls of the Assabet and look about the town before starting on
the return journey. In an hour he is in Marlboro
again, and a minute's walk will bring him to the monument, where he will take the Worcester car.

Resuming the journey on the main line, after passing by the Bigelow School, the car runs up hill and
down until Lake Williams is reached. This lake is the
source of Marlboro's water supply, and the reservoir
and standpipe are seen farther on, at the right, after
the car turns to run between the lake and St. Ann's
Convent, situated on a hill at the right. A short distance beyond the reservoir the car passes a "little red
schoolhouse" of the old-fashioned kind, opposite
which is a fine distant view of the surrounding country. The car soon passes the Rice mansion, a white-
painted building in the early colonial style of architecture, with ends of brick, and beyond is the Seaver
place, a brick house in which Edwin P. Seaver, super-
intendent of the public schools of Boston, was born.
Running past fields and woods, and passing the waiting station near Woodside Mills, the car crosses the
new Metropolitan aqueduct just completed to Southboro. At the right is the bridge which carries the
aqueduct across the Assabet River, a piece of great
engineering skill. As the car approaches

NORTHBORO, the magnificent private grounds
of Mr. Wesson, of Smith & Wesson, the widely-
known firearms manufacturers, are observed on
both sides of the road. The Gale Public Library, a
fine architectural example, is seen on the left as
Northboro village is entered. In the village church-
yard is the grave of Rabbi Judah Monis, who re-

nounced Judaism in 1722, and afterwards become
teacher of of Hebrew in Harvard College, where he
remained until his death in 1761.

WESTBORO is reached by taking a branch line
from Northboro. The line turns to the left and goes
across country, passing, on the right, the Davis Mansion, a famous resort for wheelmen and tourists, and
the Lyman School for Boys, on the hill at the left.
Westboro is the seat of a State Reform School. This
town was in the old Indian domain of Maguncook.

Again continuing on the main line from Northboro
to Worcester, the car passes the Northboro stores and
the Soldiers' Monument, and soon runs into a country
of verdant fields. Elm Tree Inn, on the right, is the
next point of interest, and then there is a long run
through a country of farms and woods, with pleasing
rural scenes on either hand, until the passenger enters

SHREWSBURY. At the entrance of the village, on the left, is the Ward Mansion, once the home
of Artemus Ward, who was a major in the siege of
Louisburg in 1758, and who commanded the American forces besieging Boston until the arrival of Washington, who made the house famous by stopping there
on his journey. The house is low and rambling, and
the great brass knocker on the door proclaims its an-
tiquity. Levi Pease, who started the first line of mail
stages between Boston and New York, in 1784, was
born here. Shrewsbury is built along a village street,
and the car runs through it, all the way up hill, at the
farther end of the street passing the Town Hall,
churches and Soldiers' Monument.

A turn to the left is soon made, and the line runs for the most part down hill with a glorious view of valley and hills beyond at the right, and Worcester visible in the distance. Soon the old turnpike is reached, and another descent brings one to Lake Quinsigamond, with its hotels, pavilions and cottages. The lake is deep and narrow, four miles long, and contains twelve islands. Here the regattas of the Worcester Boat Club, and sometimes those of the New England Association of Amateur Oarsmen, are held. Doubtless many trolley excursionists wish to stop here, and they may do so without extra charge, for at this point the car runs on the tracks of the Worcester Consolidated Street Railway Company, and another fare is taken. After leaving the lake, the electric line follows for some distance the tracks of the narrow gauge road through the fields and near the tracks of the Boston & Albany Railroad.

At the right the State Insane Asylum, a massive granite structure, is seen in the distance, and shortly after, the car turns into Shrewsbury street, and runs in a bee-line to the Union Station in Worcester. If the traveler keeps on the car to the corner of Main and Front streets, a free transfer may be had to any of the cars of the Worcester Consolidated Street Railway Company.

Two lines of the Worcester & Suburban Street Railway run westward from Worcester. One passes down the Blackstone valley for some thirteen miles, with a variety of river and hill scenery, going through Millbury, Saundersville and Rockdale, while the other goes westward over the State road to Leicester, Spencer and West Warren. Taking the Spencer car and passing the company's offices on Front street, the ride is through Portland, Southbridge, Hamlin, Canterbury and Tremont streets, there being a view from Tremont street, of Holy Cross College on the field off to the left.

At Webster Square a line diverges to Hope Cemetery and Trowbridgeville, while the main-line car runs on Main street past the Old Ladies' Home. After leaving the city, a trout hatchery is seen on the left, and at Apricot street, on the right, a mile walk brings one to a rock in the face of which is carved a deed bequeathing the surrounding country to Almighty God. Beyond Apricot street, Kettle Brook runs on the left, and Valley Falls, with its mills, is soon passed. Then the car reaches

LEICESTER, the first village in which is know as Cherry Valley. Beyond this are groves, and Waite's Pond is seen beyond the Catholic Church on the left. The car then leaves the State highway and runs on Winslow avenue, through the estate of Hon. Samuel E. Winslow, whose handsome residence is at the left, and going through Baxton street, once more enters the State road. As a turn is made to the right Leicester Common is passed, with its churches, the Town Hall and Leicester Academy.

From here the car runs down an incline, past the pretty stone Public Library Building, the street railway power house and offices, and then ascends Mount Pleasant, passing a house which was one of the inns where the Worcester and Springfield stages stopped. Just beyond here the electric car reaches an elevation of 1053 feet above sea level. Passing Burncoat Pond on the left, at the Spencer town line there is Mount Wachusett on the right as the car enters

SPENCER, which is seen in the distance. Passing through "Moose Hill Farm," owned by Rufus Sibley of Rochester, N. Y. Beyond the farm the town is in full view, and after passing Lake Whittemore and the public park on the right the car enters the village, running past the High School and near the boot factory of Isaac Prouty & Co., the largest of its kind in the world. Beyond here the line runs through a beautiful pastoral country, with many fine views of the hills, to enter Warren, beyond which is West Warren, a beautiful summer resort and the terminus of the electric line.

In addition to these lines of the Worcester & Suburban, there is a shorter line, running from the city out to North Grafton. Starting from the Union Station and crossing the railroad tracks, the line soon leaves the city behind, and on the left may be seen Flint's Pond, and then Hovey's Pond, before reaching North Grafton, where is located the home of the Worcester Country Club, with its golf links and other sporting activities. Another line will soon be in operation between Worcester and Webster.

From Worcester the main line of this journey continues to Fitchburg, a change being made to the cars of the Worcester & Clinton Street Railway either at the Railroad Station or at the City Hall, in Worcester. Soon after leaving the business district of the city, the car runs over Paine hill, from which there is a wide view of the country about. Passing the Poor Farm, on the right, the line runs across a corner of the town

of Shrewsbury. Here the ride is through a farming
country, one of the houses passed being once the
homestead of the world-famous temperance advocate,
John B. Gough. Then the car runs along through a
pleasant country to enter

BOYLSTON CENTRE, which recently cele-
brated the hundredth anniversary of its founding.
From here a view is had of Mount Wachusett, off to
the right. Boylston Centre is an interesting town,
and in the valley below lies the great Wachusett Basin
of the Metropolitan Water System, from which Boston
is to receive its water supply. The car follows along
the basin for more than three miles, and the traveler
has a good opportunity to study the great engineering
work, as the slope to the basin from the railroad tracks
is precipitous.

The view from this portion of the road is an inspiring one, with the sharp contrast of man's handiwork
with that of nature, the deep valley and the panorama
of farms and farm-houses being framed in a back-
ground of high verdure-clad hills. On the right hand
there is a screen of small trees, but the old landmark of
Wachusett is visible for a large part of the distance.
After leaving the car house in Boylston Centre, a little
school house on the left is passed, called the Seven Na-
tions School. The odd name is derived from the local
report that at one time the school had only seven pupils, representing seven different nationalities. Still
continuing through a farming country, of the New
England type, the car comes to

CLINTON, with the standpipe and reservoir on
Burdett Hill as prominent objects in the landscape.

Here the operations of the Metropolitan Water System are in a well-advanced stage. Clinton is a pretty manufacturing town and has a handsome Memorial Hall. Here a change is made to the car of the Leominster & Clinton Street Railway, which soon crosses the south branch of the Nashua River. A detour is made through the well-kept streets and past the pretty little park surrounded by churches, and the Town Hall, and then the car goes up a hill. After a pleasant ride of fifteen minutes the little village of

SOUTH LANCASTER, is reached, and a look backward gives a beautiful view of Clinton. Here are located the great estates of the Thayer family and their splendid stock farms. Before entering the town, the car leaves the public highway and runs over private property, a lease of which was given for ninety-nine years in order that the cars might not pass directly in front of the fine residence of Mr. Eugene V. R. Thayer. As the highway is entered once more the old Thayer homestead is passed on the left. It is proposed to build a branch line of street railway from this place to Hudson. Crossing the north branch of the Nashua River, the car enters

LANCASTER CENTRE, passing the Town Hall, Public Library, and church on the right, at the "north village." A little further on the north branch of the Nashua is crossed for the second time, and then the car passes the Lancaster Poor Farm on the right, and runs through a country of farms. A little further on Leominster Park is reached, a great pleasure ground on the banks of the Nashua River, maintained by the street railway company. Here may be found a bowling

alley and dining hall on one side, while across the river
is a beautiful pine grove, with a rustic theatre, situated
at the foot of an amphitheatre of rustic seats. After
leaving the park a run is made through another prosperous farming country, until

LEOMINSTER is reached. This is a busy town
with varied manufactures, important among which are
those of toys and combs, while around the town on the
line of the street railway are farms entirely devoted to
the raising of cucumbers for the markets of Boston
and New York.

From Leominster to Fitchburg a choice of routes
is open to the traveler, to less than three electric railway lines connecting these two points. The traveler
may well make the journey to Fitchburg one way, and
return by another line. Taking the car of the Fitchburg & Leominster Street Railway Co., for Fitchburg
via North Leominster, the car passes over the
Nashua River and underneath the railroad bridge,
through the pretty little village. Ascending the hill
after passing the town, one of the finest views imagina-
ble is obtained.

Nowhere in all New England can a finer farming
country be seen than from the hill which is followed all
the way from Leominster to Fitchburg. One may
have a view of the pretty town of Leominster, half
hidden in the trees, to the rear, or the long blue ranges
of hills and mountains to the left, Wachusett Mountain
and the Wanoosnucs, or the busy city of Fitchburg
ahead. A ride of a short distance brings the traveller
to Whalom Lake and Park, owned and managed by
the street railway company, and is open at all times

during the summer. It is of great natural beauty, and much has been done in displaying the natural charms of the place to the best advantage.

Whalom Lake is a beautiful sheet of water, and there is a large fleet of boats for rowing or sailing on its placid surface, and across the road from the lake is a beds of fragrant, flowering plants. An assembly hall and a dining pavilion are among the buildings, while on a rustic stage, performances are given in summer by competent artists. Merry-go-rounds, rustic seats, picnic tables, swings, a band-stand, and other attractions of a kindred nature are provided, and in the wildest part of the park is an enclosure where are kept deer, elk and moose, which are now so tame as to be easily approachable. No higher tribute can be paid to the park than the fact that picnic parties return there year after year. After leaving the park it is only a short ride to the suburbs of

FITCHBURG, the traveler still having the advantage, unusual in entering a large place, of seeing charming landscapes on every side. Rollstone Hill, seen to the left, is a picturesque feature in the landscape, and the city itself is seen in panoramic view before it is entered, and running between business blocks, the car reaches the terminus of this line in front of the American House.

Another line is by South Fitchburg, the car also leaving from the square in Leominster, and is the most direct between the two places. The route is through the little village of South Fitchburg, passing the Fitchburg Almshouse and County Jail on the left. A ride of thirty minutes from Leominster brings one

into Fitchburg, the terminus. This city, with its busy
manufactures and its wide-awake population, contains
much that is of interest to the visitor. Several local
lines of street railway pass out of Fitchburg, one of the
most interesting rides being that on the line to West
Fitchburg, which passes by Rollstone Hill, where are
located the famous Fitchburg granite quarries, and
from which there are views of wide extent.

Up the Mystic Valley.

FROM Boston a line of cars runs up the beautiful valley of the Mystic River, and this is soon to be continued from North Woburn, its present terminus, through Wilmington and Tewksbury to Lowell, passing Silver Lake, near Lowell, one of the prettiest little lakes in Eastern Massachusetts. Two routes from Boston are offered to the traveler who wishes to make this journey along the Mystic River. One is by way of Medford, the excursionist taking a Medford car at Scollay Square or the North Station, and running out through Charlestown and over Winter Hill, on the route of Paul Revere's historic ride. The other is a longer trip, and the passenger takes an Arlington car in the Subway or at Scollay Square, on the surface. The ride to Arlington is through Cambridge, the car passing through Harvard Square, with the college buildings on the right, and then running out Massachusetts Avenue through North Cambridge to Arlington. Here a change is made to the car of the Arlington & Winchester Street Railway, and the line turns to the right, between the hills, and soon the beautiful Mystic lakes are seen on the right, before the car enters

WINCHESTER, a pretty town, with many old residences, and more of the modern ones, where dwell many Boston business men. On the high hills to the east of the town is the Middlesex Fells Reservation, which is passed on the other side in another trip to Lowell. From Winchester a branch line runs to

STONEHAM, going through a picturesque rural country before reaching this busy shoe manufacturing village. From here cars run to Melrose, Wake-

RESIDENCE OF COL. BALDWIN WHO FOUGHT AT LEXINGTON
AND AT THE SIEGE OF BOSTON.

field, Reading and Woburn, Woburn Square being the centre for all the car lines entering the city. The Woburn car from Winchester runs northward, passing many pretty bits of scenery along the Mystic River, which is but a small stream compared with the swelling river at its mouth. The car runs past farms and market gardens before entering

WOBURN, which is noted for its great tanneries and leather industries. It also contains much that is of historic interest, and has a handsome public Library building, with other than bookish attractions. Going from here to North Woburn, one passes, on the left, the Baldwin place, where the famous Baldwin apples originated, and farther on, as the car enters

NORTH WOBURN, it goes by the home of Benjamin Thompson, Count Rumford, the famous physicist and philosopher. The house is seen on the

BIRTHPLACE OF COUNT RUMFORD WITH ITS OLD WELL SWEEP.

left. From Woburn the car runs across country again to Reading, going by houses of the old Colonial style and handsome villas of modern architecture. For the greater part of the trip the ride is through a pretty farming country. The car passes, on the way, the famous Walnut Hill Rifle Range, the home of the Massachusetts Rifle Association. Entering

READING, the car goes through the best part of the town, where many Boston men live. Within a short time an electric car line will be completed from

Woburn to Lowell, going directly to Wilmington and running by a more direct route than the other one mentioned. It will also afford an opportunity to visit Silver Lake, where the street railway company will establish a pleasure park. The lake is already visited by many excursionists from Lowell, and when the facilities for reaching it are increased, it is sure to be patronized by thousands of pleasure-seekers, as the natural beauties of the place are of the highest order.

From Boston to Lowell.

O NE may ride on the electric cars from Boston
through Lowell, clear to Nashua, N. H., while
there is a line running from Lowell down the
Merrimack Valley to the sea. Taking a Malden car
in the Subway or at the North Union Station, where
it emerges from under ground, the line crosses the
Charles River and runs through Charlestown, past
Bunker Hill Monument, on the right, to Sullivan
Square. Here it turns to the right and runs across
Mystic Bridge, from which there are fine views of the
wide mouth of the Mystic River, with Winter Hill
off on the left. Then the car runs through Everett,
up hill and down, soon coming into Malden Square,

MALDEN, where there is a notable group of
fine buildings. One of these is the First Baptist
Church, another the High School and the third the
brownstone Memorial Building, containing a Public
Library and an art gallery, the gift of E. S. Converse,
who also contributed to the erection of the other
buildings. Changing at Malden Square to a Melrose
car, on the Lynn & Boston Street Railway, the way
leads out of the populated part of the city past Pine
Banks Park on the right, a pleasure ground open to
the people of Malden and Melrose, and another
monument to the noble philanthropy of Mr. Converse,

who here arranged one of the finest private pleasure
grounds in the country. A little beyond the park,
on the other side, may be seen the great works of
the Boston Rubber Shoe Company at the foot of the
Middlesex Fells Reservation, one of the great state
parks. Leaving Fells Station, the car enters

MELROSE, passing the Town Hall and pretty
Ell Pond. At Melrose Highlands the passenger
changes to the cars of the Wakefield and Stoneham
Street Railway. The car runs through the pretty
little village of Greenwood, with its many market
gardens, passing the Greenwood School on the right
and the railroad station on the left. Beyond here is
Crystal Lake, its banks bordered by attractive residences. As the car enters

WAKEFIELD, the Wakefield Home for Children is passed, on the right, and then, on the same
side, the great Wakefield Rattan Works, the principal
industry. From Wakefield cars may be taken to
Lynn and also to Stoneham, an important shoe manufacturing town. A line also runs to Peadody passing Suntaug Park. Leaving the city, the car runs in
the direction of Salem to North Saugus, on the route
to Lynn Woods. Here a turn is made to the left,
and a short run brings one to Lynnfield, within sight
of Suntaug Pond, on the shore of which the street
railway park is located. Before it was improved it
was popular with picnic parties, on account of its
clear water and wooded shores, but it has been
cleaned up and buildings have been erected. There
is a large bicycle stall at the entrance, and a dining
hall and dancing pavilion near the centre of the

park, while there is a picnic house with tables, and a boathouse on the lake, where may be found a fleet of rowboats and an electric launch. A free open-air theatre is largely patronized and vaudeville performances are given every afternoon and evening on week days, with Sunday evening concerts. Beyond the park the line runs through a rural country into Peabody, described elsewhere in this Guide. At Wakefield a change is made to the cars of the Reading & Lowell Street Railway. After passing the Town Hall and post office, the car runs past the Common in Wakefield, located on Lake Quannapowitt, a beautiful sheet of water, dotted with yachts and other small pleasure boats.

WAKEFIELD PUBLIC PARK.

Along the shores of this lake the car runs for nearly two miles, turning in and out, and affording many delightful views. A run of a mile from the lake brings one to Reading Square, in

READING, from which the standpipe and Pumping Station of the waterworks are seen on the right. Passing up Lowell Street and by the Reading Cemetery, the car goes by the Reading Grammar School. Leaving the town, the ride is through rural country for some distance, and then the car enters the residence district of

WILMINGTON, passing the Wilmington Cemetery and the Walker School. Leaving the pretty little town, it is a short run into the open country again, where the car strikes the towpath of the almost forgotten Middlesex Canal, which connected Boston and Lowell by a waterway in the early part of the century. The picturesque and grass-grown wasteways are seen at intervals. At Silver Street a walk to the right brings one to another Silver Lake,

SHAWSHEEN RIVER.

a popular summer resort. Following the canal through the country, cattle are seen grazing peacefully on the towpath, while the electric car takes one over one of the largest cranberry bogs in the state, and soon comes to the swift running Shawsheen River, where the massive gray stone piers on the right are all that is left of what was once the great double lock of the canal. After a ride through fragrant pines and country roads, the car goes through East Billerica and then past the Billerica Cemetery and after a run through more woods reaches an elevation from which, in clear weather, Mount Tom and Mount Wachusett in Massachusetts and Mount Monadnock in New Hampshire may be seen, while there is a fine nearer view of Lowell and its vicinity. In the little village of

BILLERICA, a change is made to the cars of the Lowell and Suburban Street Railway, which soon pass the Howe School and the residence of Senator Joshua B. Holden. The car then runs through more fields and forests, with glimpses of the Concord River, and past a weather-beaten house marked by a tablet as the former home of Asa Pollard, the first man to fall at Bunker Hill. Crossing the Concord River, and running through North Billerica, with its great Talbot Chemical Works, the car goes through North Chelmsford and enters

LOWELL. After passing the Fair Grounds and the Butler School, on the right, the car runs on Gorham Street, between the handsome new Court House and the large Catholic Church. Farther down the Street, the car passes the postoffice and Federal Building on the left, and runs into Merrimack Square, stopping in front of the Runels Building, the terminus for all the car lines entering Lowell.

In going from Lowell to Nashua the line runs across the Merrimac River, affording a fine view of the great cotton mills, and soon reaches Lakeview Park, a popular summer resort, where are many attractions for travelers, a spacious pavilion, a Zoological garden, a fleet of boats, and a steamer on the lake, in addition to the usual park conveniences. From the park the line runs through the woods and field, past farms and pastures, crossing the river once more before entering the New Hampshire city of Nashua.

In addition to the various lines out of the city, described elsewhere, there are many pleasant rides in the city of Lowell itself. The Pawtucket car takes

one through the business district and up the bank
of the Merrimac; the Westford Street car takes one
to Lowell Highlands, from which there is a wide
view, but the most extensive view can be had by
taking a Fort Hill Park car running through Belvidere and the fine residence district to Fort Hill Park,
from the summit of which there is a view for miles in
every direction.

MOUNTAIN ROCK PARK, LAKEVIEW,

Down the Merrimac Valley.

A LONG the route of the electric cars, down the Merrimac Valley, the ride is through a country made famous by the pen of Whittier, and which in addition to natural charms, presents a succession of busy cities and towns. The start is from Merrimac square and Bridge street, in Lowell, the car running between the great cotton mills for which the city is world-famous. The view of the mills at dusk, with their mile of lighted windows, is a striking one. After crossing the river, the car runs along the high bank. after turning to the right, giving a good view of Hunt's Falls.

Across the river is the beautiful residence district of Lowell, Belvidere. Passing through Ellsmere, in the town of Dracut, there is a view of Tewksbury, over the river, and as the car runs through the little hamlet of Kenwood and reaches Varnum's Landing, the Hood Stock Farm is seen on the other side. This is a favorite summer resort, and has a little ferry, and a steamer line running to Lawrence. The car leaves the thoroughfare to run along the river bank over private property for eight miles before coming to Glen Forest, on the right, a pleasure park for the people of Lowell and Lawrence. The wooded shores, smooth waters and pine groves are supplemented by attractions pro-. vided by the Lowell, Lawrence & Haverhill Street Railway Co., which owns the park. The place is especially noted for its holiday fireworks displays. It is only a short run from here to

GLEN FOREST.

LAWRENCE, one of the greatest cotton manufacturing cities in the world. Among its mills one alone employs 3600 operatives. A great canal runs through the city, the Merrimac River furnishing water power by means of a dam a thousand feet long and twenty-eight feet fall. Lawrence is a great railway' centre, with side lines to Methuen, North Andover and Andover, in addition to the city lines and the main line down the Merrimac Valley.

The car to Andover starts from the corner of Broadway and Essex streets, and passes, on the left, the Pacific Mills, and as the river is crossed, affords a fine view of the dam. Running through South Lawrence, with its stone-cutting and other industries, the state highway is traversed from the Andover line, through Frye Village and over the Shawshine River with its factories. As the car enters

ANDOVER, it passes the Post Office, Memorial Hall, and the Public Library, in Andover Square. The town was founded in 1643, and passed through the terror of Indian warfare and the Salem Witchcraft. Yet it has been a place of learning. Beyond the square are the buildings and grounds of Abbott Seminary, founded in 1829, and on Main street, at No. 147, "America" was written. The buildings of Phillips Andover Academy, founded in 1778, are on the right, and on the left is the Andover Theological Seminary, founded in 1808. Near by is the Mansion House, once the home of Harriet Beecher Stowe.

NORTH ANDOVER is reached by another electric line from Lowell, the car crossing the river some distance below the dam. Here are the houses which were the homes of Anne Bradstreet, the first poet of the Merrimac Valley, Moody Bridges of the First Provincial Congress, Dr. Thos. Kittredge, and six succeeding generations of physicians, and Phillips Brooks, Wendell Phillips and Dr. Oliver Wendell Holmes.

METHUEN is on a third line of electric cars from Lawrence. The town rises on the hills back of Lawrence, and the summit is crowned by the Nevins Memorial Library and a Soldiers and Sailors' Monument given to the town by C. H. Tenney, whose fine estate, "Greycourt," is here. In the First Church is LaFarge's masterpiece, "The Resurrection Morning."

Resuming the journey down the Merrimac, a change is made at the corner of Broadway and Essex street, to the Haverhill car, the way leading past the Common, the City Hall and Court House on the left and through the business district. Crossing the Spicket River the car goes through a corner of Methuen.

Going through Kenwood Village, the car passes the great Russell Celery farm, from which a good view is had of Ward Hill in Bradford, on the right. Following the river, the old red barn on the Bradley Farm, once a tavern, is passed, and running past Bradford Neck and Mitchell's Falls the car enters

HAVERHILL, reaching the terminus at Washington Square. This is the centre for all cars running out of the city, for besides the line down the river, there are branches to Georgetown and West Newbury, which may well be taken up before continuing on the main line. Taking a car at the corner of Bridge and Merrimac streets, the route is across the Merrimac to Ward's Hill, and then into the town of

BRADFORD, passing the old Bradford Common to the right Then the car runs by the old cemetery and the Peabody School on the left. In Bradford is an academy for girls, occupying a commanding site on a hill. Founded in 1803, this institution has been noted as a nursery of foreign missionaries and missionaries' wives. Here, also, is the Dudley Carleton House, used for prisoners in the Revolution. From Temple Hill there is a fine view of the Merrimac and Haverhill. Continuing on, there is a pleasant ride through meadows into

SOUTH GROVELAND, where a road leads from Parker's corner to Johnson's Pond. To take this ride it is necessary to walk a short distance to the little steamer which will take one to the Grove, a great pleasure resort, with provision for boating and other outdoor sports, concerts and theatrical entertainments.

From South Groveland the car runs through two miles or more of woodland in the centre of which is a beautiful little lake called Rock Pond, covered with pond lilies, and teeming with pickerel and black bass. From this leads a little stream into another lake called Pentucket Pond, which may be seen to the left after passing the Weston crossing of the Boston & Maine Railroad. This lake is surrounded by a beautiful growth of pines called Yacht Club Grove, where are a pavilion, dancing hall and private picnic grounds. Beyond this comes

GEORGETOWN, the terminus of the line which will be extended south ultimately to connect with North Shore lines. This is a manufacturing town, making boots, shoes and carriages. It was one of the main stations on the old road from Danvers to Newburyport. On the ride from Haverhill down the South bank of the river to West Newbury and Newburyport the car runs past the old Spiller Garrison house on the left, built in 1690, out of bricks brought from England.

Beyond, on the left, is the old Powder House, built in the war of 1812. Then comes the almshouse on the right, and then the car passes Riverside Park and goes over the river, where the steamer takes on its passengers from the opened drawbridge. Going into

GROVELAND, the car passes Perry Park on the left, and then, on the Merrimac banks, comes to the great pleasure ground known as the Pines. Here are boats, swings, a dancing hall, pavilion, and an electrical fountain. Here a change is made to another line which runs to

WEST NEWBURY. Off to the right is Brown's Hill, from which may be seen a panorama of farms and villages, while the eye may follow the broad Merrimac until it is lost in the dim blue of the Atlantic, as it runs on into Newburyport, the terminus.

HAVERHILL, founded in 1640, and now second only to Lynn in the manufacture of shoes, is best seen by taking the electric line running to Merrimac. Boarding the car in Washington Square, the line runs through the residence district into Monument Square, past the Soldiers' Monument, the Universalist Church and the residence of Edward Gale, who gave to the city Gale Park, on the right bordering on Lake Saltonstall.

Beyond here the car passes Kenoza Lake, on the right, on which is another city park. On the opposite side of the park the car passes the Haverhill City Hospital and the city Pumping Station. Beyond, on the left, is Kenoza Trotting Park, and running on, to Columbia Heights, the highest point of land in Essex County, there is a glorious view of the Merrimac Valley.

Leaving the lake on the left of the electric line is the homestead where John G. Whittier, the poet, dwelt, the original house which is pictured in "Snow Bound," preserved today almost as it was in Whittier's time, by the Whittier Memorial Society of Haverhill. It is a short ride to Sanders Hill, with a grand view of New Hampshire scenery off to the north. Running over Tucker's Hill, with another beautiful view, the car goes through Main Street into Merrimac Square.

MERRIMAC. From here there are two lines to the sea. Going on to Salisbury Beach the car climbs

WHITTIER'S BIRTHPLACE.

Pond Hill, from which the stock farm of E. Moody Boynton, inventor of the bicycle railroad, is seen on the right, in West Newbury. Halfway down the hill is the Thomas Chellis house, built in 1695, and from the street railway turnout just beyond a road runs off to Lake Attitash, a popular summer resort. Passing the castle built by Sir Edward Thornton, on the right, and going by the Union Cemetery, where Whittier is buried, the line runs into the highlands of

AMESBURY, the home of the poet from 1840 until his death. From here a line runs to Seabrook

Hampton, Hampton Beach and Exeter, N. H. In going to these places it is best to take the cars at Market Square in Amesbury. The passenger is carried along Market street, and a turn to the right takes one past the car house of the company. At the next turn, which is to the left, the line runs into the open country, with its well-kept houses and beautiful farms. Crossing a part of Salisbury, the car

PARKER HOUSE, SEABROOK.

enters the pretty little village of Seabrook, where the line from Newburyport also comes in. Coming into the old post road between Newburyport and Exeter, one passes, on the left, the old Parker House, a famous old road house which is now much frequented by bicycle riders and trolley excursionists. A little beyond here is a neat white house, on the right, where Whittier once lived. Then the car runs into the pretty village of Hampton Falls, after leaving which a fine view is had of Hampton Beach, off to the left over the marshes. As the car enters

HAMPTON, it passes the General Moulton house and the Tappan or Garrison house and runs between the giant oaks which furnish shade much of the way, into the little square where the Whittier Hotel, known in the stage coach days as the Union House, is located. This was the half-way house of the stage line from Newburyport to Portsmouth.

From this point a line runs off to the right to Hampton Beach, a ride of some three miles over the shore. Hampton Beach is a famous one, and as the car enters it, the Great Boar's Head, that curious natural formation, and the life-saving station, are seen off to the left. The street railway company is making an extension to this line, and before the end of this summer will run over the extreme end of Hampton Beach to Boar's Head, nearly five miles along the water's edge. The company is also building a large pavilion in which there will be a dancing hall, bowling alley, dining room, etc., with a thousand square feet of verandas on the first and second stories.

From Hampton to Exeter the ride is a pleasant one, passing through a prosperous farming country with beautiful landscapes on either side. The distance is about eight miles, and after going through the rural scenery of the New Hampshire seacoast, the car enters

EXETER, in which the immense oaks are everywhere prominent. The car runs to the railroad

station, which is considered the terminus, although
the line makes a circuit of the city. Passing the railroad station, and then going by the famous Phillips
Exeter Academy, one of the oldest and most important of the American preparatory schools; the
Town Hall and Public Library and the Court House,
located on a square, giving one an excellent idea of
Exeter and its public institutions.

Amesbury is a great carriage manufacturing town,
and after passing the Hamilton Mills on the way to
Salisbury Beach the car goes over carriage Hill, past
the factories, and by the Friends' Meeting House and
soon enters

SALISBURY, where the Passaconaway Indians
once held great feasts, as is attested by heaps of
clam shells. The car runs on through East Salisbury to

SALISBURY BEACH, which, with its six-mile
strip of sand, offers some of the best bathing on the
Atlantic Coast. From the broad veranda of the
Cushing Hotel may be seen the Hampton River and
the Isle of Shoals.

From Amesbury, as well as from Merrimac, elec-
trics run to Newburyport and Newbury Old Town.
Taking a car at Market Square, in Amesbury, the
route passes, on the left, "The Captain's Well."

Passing through a farming country, the car goes
by the brick Old Ladies' Home, on the left, the birthplace of Josiah Bartlett. Crossing the Merrimac, the
car runs along the banks and recrosses on the "Chain
Bridge," erected in 1792 and replaced in 1810. On
Deer Island, over which the bridge runs, is the home

of Harriett Prescott Spofford.   Passing the old ship-
yards, the car soon runs into

NEWBURYPORT, at the mouth of the Merrimac, reaching the terminus at Market Square, near
which was the home of "Goody Morse," convicted of
witchcraft.   On the ride to Newbury Old Town, the
car taken at the corner of State and Pleasant streets
passes the Catholic Burying Ground on the left, Atkin-
son Common, the Home for Aged Men, the Pillsbury

CHAIN BRIDGE.

Place, once the home of Edward Rawson, secretary of
the Massachusetts Bay Colony for many years, and
the home of Lord Timothy Dexter.

In Brown Square, given to the city by Moses
Brown, in 1802, is the statue of William Lloyd Garri-
son.   The City Hall is across the street.   Before turn-
ing into State street the car passes the meeting house
of the First Religious Society.   The car goes by the
Public Library, once the Tracy House, the Y. M. C.
A. building and the Whitefield Congregational
Church.   Turning into High street there is a view of

Washington Park, on the right. Along High street the car runs into

NEWBURY OLD TOWN, passing the Ilsley House, built in 1670, and coming to "Trayneing Green," on the right. Here camped the soldiers in the Quebec Expedition under Benedict Arnold in 1775, and beyond on the left may be seen the chimneys of the Spencer-Pierce House, also called the Garrison House. Newbury Old Town has had many famous citizens. The terminus of the line is at Oldtown, a pretty summer resort on the Parker River.

OLD SOUTH CHURCH, NEWBURYPORT

PLUM ISLAND is reached by another electric line from Newburyport. The cars, from Market Square, pass a stone post at Middle and Independence streets, on which is a bombshell brought from Louisburg. At School street the Old South Church is passed, under which is buried the great preacher George Whitefield. Next to the church is the house where William Lloyd Garrison was born, and it is only a short run from here over the marshes to Plum Island.

Through the Lake Region.

FROM Bridgewater southward a line runs through the lake region of Massachusetts to the interesting city of New Bedford. The route after leaving the town of Bridgewater, runs through a farming country, with old farmhouses along the way and glimpses of meadow, field and forest scenery. After crossing Sawmill Brook and the Taunton River, the car enters

TITICUT, where the Massachusetts State Farm is one of the principal attractions. There are many fine residences in the town, which is a favorite resort for sportsmen. Leaving this and running through North Middleboro, which is devoted largely to shoe manufacture, the car goes on into

MIDDLEBORO, a prosperous town with varied manufactures, an academy, a handsome Town Hall and a Public Library building. East of here are the great Plymouth Woods, while the journey goes southward between the great Lakeville Ponds. Soon after leaving the town the car comes to

LAKEVILLE, within sight of Assawompsett Pond, which is the largest body of fresh water in the state, comprising from six to eight square miles. On the shores of this pond Captain Dermer was received by the Wampanoag Indian sachems in 1619, and here the treacherous Chief Corbitant after revolting against Massasoit in 1621, siezed the Plymouth

envoys, and was punished by an expedition from
Plymouth under Miles Standish.   South of Assawompsett is Great Quittacus Pond, while on the
other side of the electric railway, stretching along for
several miles, is Long Pond.   The ponds all abound
in fish, and the ride along their banks on the electric
cars is a beautiful one.   On the shores of this pond
the street railway company has established a park,
which is now in process of improvement.   The park
is surrounded by attractive landscapes, with the
sandy shores of the lake affording an opportunity for
fresh water bathing, while there are groves, swings,
rustic benches, a dining pavilion, merry-go-rounds,
two band stands, a rustic theatre, a bowling alley,
and as a special feature, provision for water polo, for
diving and other aquatic sports, while a fleet of
boats will be put on the lake.   Going on from the
park the railway runs through another farming country, along the Acushnet River and through the
village of Acushnet coming into

NEW BEDFORD, a famous old seaport which
has much of interest to show the visitor.   This was
once the greatest whaling port in the world.   This
was a "nest of privateers" in the revolution, and the
town was burned by a British force under Clinton in
1778.   The old whaling wharve are well worth a
visit.   There are several electric car rides in New-
edford, one of the most interesting being that to

FAIRHAVEN and old Fort Phoenix, situated
out on the point of land which guards the harbor.
The ride is a pleasant one, and near the terminus
passes the splendid grounds and residence of Henry
H. Rogers, the Standard Oil magnate.

A. H. DAVENPORT,

MANUFACTURER OF

FURNITURE AND HOUSE

FINISH

Importer of English and French

Curtain · and · Upholstery · Stuffs.

English and French WALL PAPERS

---

96 and 98 Washington Street, Boston.

331 Fifth Avenue, New York.

. *Rowley* .

Contains many sights of interest. It was settled in 1638, by a nomadic church led by EZEKIEL ROGERS, who had been the non-conformist pastor of a church in Rowley, England. The pastor of the church, upon his death in 1650, left his library to Harvard College. The first cloth made in America was turned out in the mills erected by these immigrants. Today the town is principally noted for the manufacture of canoes. Here is located the manufacturing establishment of

C. B. Mather & Co.

On Depot Street,

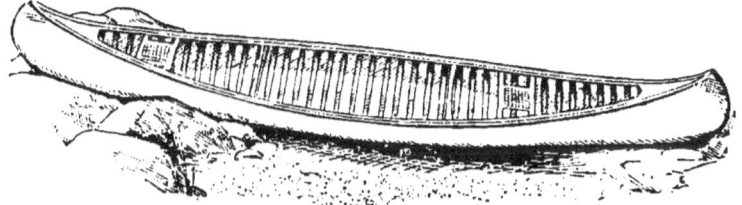

where are turned out, annually,
hundreds of

Canoes and Boats.

The business is rapidly growing, and the firm has been obliged to increase its facilities recently by the addition of a new shop 100 feet long, which, with the original establishment, will be devoted exclusively to the manufacture of boats and canoes, to be sent from here to all parts of the world, another triumph of Yankee enterprise and skill. An electric line will shortly be in operation from Rowley across the Parker River and go past Byfield to Newburyport or to Georgetown and Haverhill.

Manganese Steel

SPECIAL WORK

Proven under the Severest Service in the Tracks of the
Boston Elevated Railway Company
to be the LONGEST WEARING SPECIAL WORK NOW MADE.

Manufactured only by

Wm. Wharton, Jr. & Co., Inc.

Works, 25th St. and Washington Ave.

Philadelphia, Penn.

Harrington, Robinson & Co.

272-276 FRANKLIN STREET

BOSTON, MASS.

NEW ENGLAND AGENTS.

ALSO

Rails, Splice Bars, Bolts, Spikes, Etc.

Everything for Street Railway Track and
Overhead Construction.

We have Complete Stock of Spikes, Track Bolts, Etc.

The Only Stock in Boston from which deliveries can be made at any
hour of the day to any wharf, railroad or express.

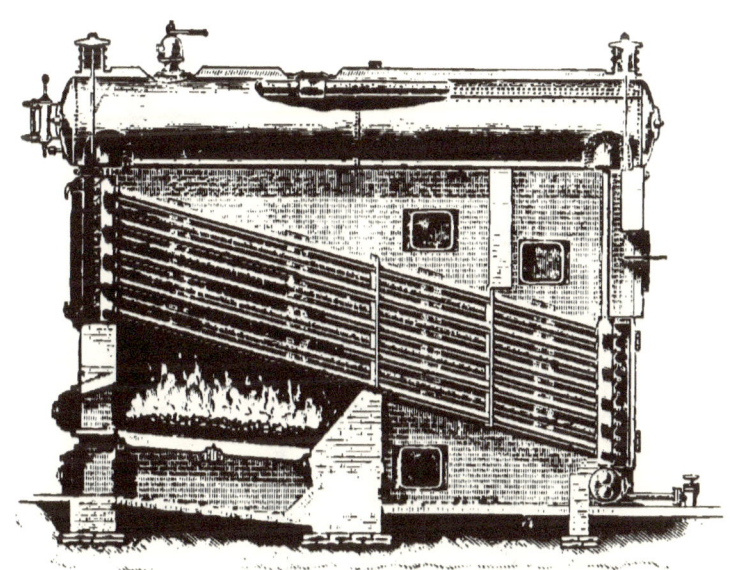

GO TO

NORUMBEGA
PARK

The Finest Trolley Trip
The Best Excursion
The Most Perfect Roads for Bicylists

Read description inside:-pages 66 to 72